THREEFOLD

(Unlikely Lovers – Book 2)

by

SOTIA LAZU

Love doesn't need to be defined, to rock your world.
Let it.

Table of Contents

Colin

Chapter One

"Really? Her?" Colin cocked his head to the right and narrowed his eyes at the young woman across the street. Nope. Even from this angle, she looked a little too round for his tastes. Her dark, curly hair a little too messy. Her brown eyes a little too plain.

"I like her." Brad shrugged. "She's fun."

"They all are."

"She's different. And she's sexy."

"Doesn't sexy usually come with a waistline?"

"Smart is sexy."

"You can't fuck *smart*."

Brad shook his head. "You're an ass."

"You just now realized that?"

"I keep hoping you'll surprise me. I should know better."

"You really should. But don't worry. I'll be nice."

Brad chuckled. "Oh, I'm not worried. She can handle you."

Before Colin could ask exactly what that meant, the light turned green, and she walked toward them. Her gaze fell on Brad, and her full lips parted to reveal perfect white teeth. Colin thought he saw a flash of whatever had his best friend so hooked on her. Her smile seemed to spread from her mouth to her eyes, and for an instant, she was beautiful.

Still, she could use a makeover.

She reached them and gave Brad a brief kiss. She turned to Colin, and he saw her eyes weren't just brown after all, but filled with green specks.

"You must be Colin the Scoundrel." She smiled again and held out her hand.

Colin got the distinct impression she wasn't joking, despite the lightness of her tone. Unfazed, he returned her smile and took her palm in his. "Nice to meet you, Becca."

Her shake was surprisingly firm. She held both his gaze and his hand a heartbeat longer, then winked. "We'll see how you feel after lunch."

"Italian?" Brad asked.

"Don't care, as long as it's nearby. I'm hungry."

Instead of saying something snarky, Colin found himself following the couple and stealing a glance at Becca's ass, which swished with every step. Sizeable but round, it stretched her jeans nicely.

Nicely?

Brad was getting to him, and Colin needed to hook up with a tall, hot blonde, before he dropped his standards like his friend obviously had.

* * * *

Becca blew her hair out of eyes, but a single curl kept falling forward. She huffed and tucked it behind one ear.

Across the table, Colin watched her trail her manicured fingers down one side of her neck, and wondered if the gesture was consciously sensual.

She rolled her shoulders and tossed the menu on the table. "I'll have a Caprese salad," she said. "And any creamy pasta they got. I skipped breakfast."

"Yeah, I can tell you look malnourished." Brad grinned, his dark chocolate eyes twinkling with mischief.

Colin didn't know why he didn't find it funny; it was definitely something he might say, if he weren't on his best behavior.

Becca laughed. "I do, don't I?" She pulled Brad to her by the collar of his Polo shirt, and ran the tip of her tongue along his lower lip. "I might have to eat you too," she whispered, but Colin heard.

And he got hard.

And there was something seriously wrong with him.

He squirmed in his seat and cleared his throat. "So, Becca, Brad tells me you're a painter."

She sat back. "I am."

"What are your influences?" And could he have sounded more pretentious?

"Houses in need of color." She delivered the words straight-faced, but Brad chortled.

"She's not *that* kind of painter, you douche."

Becca's right hand disappeared under the table — probably on Brad's thigh. "Don't be mean. It's an easy mistake to make. I totally look the starving-artist type."

Colin let out a bark of laughter before he could stop himself. Becca scowled at him, and he felt like an ass. "I'm sorry. I didn't—"

"Dude, I'm messing with you," she said, her face breaking into that radiant smile. "I'm fully aware I look neither starved nor artistic, and I'm cool with it. Now breathe, and tell me how you and Brad met. I never asked, and you know how forthcoming this one generally is with information about himself."

Colin still felt bad, but took the out she gave him. "I sold his mother a house six years ago. She was on a business trip when the papers were supposed to be signed, and Brad was her proxy. After the sale was finalized, we went for a beer."

"Or ten." Brad motioned for the waitress. "The lady will have an insalata Caprese and a spaghetti Carbonara, and I'll have a spaghetti Bolognese."

The leggy blonde jotted that down and turned to Colin. "And you, sir?"

"He'll have a mixed salad, but what he really wants is your number," Brad answered. "The poor guy is recently single and has been mooning over you since we sat down."

Colin hadn't even noticed her before, but now he did, he wouldn't mind getting her number… or anything else of hers that was on offer. Her high heels brought her to just shy of six feet, and she was slim, with narrow hips and small, perky breasts. He could tell she wasn't wearing a bra.

"I don't know… I'm not allowed to go out with customers." She studied Colin's face, and he tried to keep his expression as innocent as possible.

Suddenly, Becca smacked her forehead. "Oh my God, Jules. I can't believe I didn't recognize you. Remember me? Becca? From that thing last year?"

The waitress seemed confused. "I—"

"Come on, that *thing*. With the food? You were with what's-her-face, and we said we'd meet up, but you never called. Bet you've lost my number, huh?" Before the woman could reply, Becca brought out a cell-phone. "You give me yours this time."

Reluctantly, the waitress did just that.

"Shit. I can't remember how to write your last name. Spell it for me?"

"You can't remember how to spell Bell?"

"Heh. Brain-glitch." Becca waggled her eyebrows. "Thanks Jules. I'll make sure to call you. Nice running into you."

"Um… you too. I'll be right back with your order."

"You don't know her, do you?" Brad said, as soon as the waitress was out of sight.

"Never seen her before in my life."

He gave her a smacking kiss on the lips. "You make me so hot when you're naughty."

"Down boy." She was smiling as she handed Colin the cell she held. "Here. All ready for you."

It was his phone.

"How did you…?"

"Her nametag read Julia. It wasn't a huge leap from there. The trick is to talk fast—not give them much time to think and notice the holes in your story."

"There was nothing *but* holes in your story, but I meant my phone. How did you get it from my back pocket?"

"I have very nimble fingers." She waggled them, and Colin shook his head.

She *was* fun.

"Are you really recently single?" Becca asked.

"Can't you see he's heartbroken?"

Colin mock-glared at Brad. "Wasn't in a relationship to begin with."

"At least that's his story. Helga saw things differently, hence the parting of ways when she caught him with someone else."

"*Helga?*"

"Flight attendant," Brad supplied, ever so helpful.

"Of course."

"Of course?" Colin asked.

"It fits the picture Brad has painted of your character. You know—serial model-type dater with commitment issues."

The way her eyes glinted with mirth, Colin couldn't take offence. Not that he would otherwise. The description fit. "That's me in a nutshell."

She seemed to really study him for a moment. "Maybe."

There was something undoubtedly magnetic about her gaze, and Colin decided he liked her. In the completely platonic way one could like his best friend's chubby girlfriend.

"I'm just wondering whom you'd cheat on Helga the Flight Attendant with," she said. "Swimsuit model?"

Colin hung his head.

"Victoria's Angel?" Becca asked.

He hid his face in his hands.

"Barista," Brad said. "But she wants to be an actor."

Becca tapped her chin with her index finger. "Huh. I don't know if I'd ever sleep with an actor. I'd be wondering if he was really into it or playing a part. Weren't you worried?"

"Hadn't thought about it till just now," Colin said.

"Well, now you can, and it's all 'cause of me. Glad to have been of service."

Brad messed Becca's curly mop of hair even more, and she grinned. Dimples appeared on her cheeks.

For the first time, Colin wondered if maybe smart *was* sexy.

If maybe Becca was sexy.

It wasn't the last time he wondered that.

The thought crossed his mind again when Becca's pasta arrived, and she closed the perfect *O* her lips formed over her first bite. Her eyelids drifted shut, and she let out an appreciative moan that sent a vibration all the way down Colin's spine. He could easily imagine hearing that sound in bed, muffled by soft, smooth thighs pressing against his ears. He wasn't thinking of *Becca* rolling in his silken sheets and making those sounds, of course. Just some random fuck.

Of course.

He really was a piece of shit.

"So, how did you two get together?" He needed to be reminded that they very much *were* together.

Brad said, "We—"

"Long story." Becca stuffed her mouth with more spaghetti and looked away. There was definitely a story there.

"I have nowhere to be for a couple hours." Colin sat back and steepled his fingers.

"Okay," Becca said. "We met online."

"Like in a chat-room?"

Brad let his head fall back. "Sort of."

"It was a sex ad, two months ago. You know, in Personals? I'd posted about needing to get laid, and Brad promised me a good nine inches of wood. The liar."

Brad's head snapped back up, and Colin choked on his water.

"Seriously?" he asked.

"No, man." Brad raked his fingers through his midnight-black hair. "I was looking for someone to paint the second bedroom. And you're a sick fuck."

"Sticks and stones."

Becca laughed. She was quick to laugh. Colin liked that too. He also liked the way her breasts bounced when she laughed. And Brad was right; he was a sick fuck.

"Can't believe you fell for that," Becca said.

"You totally look the type of gal to get her jollies from strangers," Brad said.

"Eh, not lately." She said it with a smile, but Colin got the impression she wasn't all that happy about it.

"But you'd do it?" he asked. "Sleep with a stranger?"

"Brad and I hadn't exactly exchanged social security numbers when we first…"

"Yeah, but there was no sleeping, either."

Becca pinched his cheek. "You stud, you. No, this good Catholic boy lost at least half his Heaven-cred that night."

Brad preened, and Colin shook his head. This was the first time he saw Brad being so casual about his sex life. The guy was usually a prude. Whatever else Becca might be, she was freeing his best friend, and Colin decided to like her for that alone.

Only, for a heartbeat, he thought he might like her for more than that.

That night, he fucked Jules the waitress in a hotel room. She was limber, and way more active in bed than really beautiful women usually were.

She rolled off him with a satisfied sigh. "Well, that was refreshing."

"Indeed." Colin traced the outline of her ribcage, getting ready for the I-don't-usually-do-these-things speech. He knew the song and dance. None of them *usually* jumped in bed with a stranger, but they made an exception just for him. Some blamed it on his dark blue eyes, some on the body he spent hours maintaining. He knew the truth. He was a hunter, and he could find the chink in anyone's armor. Once he chipped away enough of an opening for himself, nobody turned him down.

"This hotel is so lovely. I've never been here before." She smiled.

The answer to her unspoken question was that yes, he visited the place a lot. It was clean, luxurious, close to home, and most of all, had a discreet staff that didn't bat an eyelid, no matter who joined Colin in his usual room. He didn't tell Jules that. "It has great room service. Hungry?" He wasn't an animal. Just because he didn't care for a relationship, didn't mean he treated women badly.

"I could eat." Her smile faltered when he jumped out of bed and passed her the menu from the nightstand.

He pulled off his condom, tied a knot in it, and tossed it in the garbage can by the dresser. "Order anything you want. It's on me."

She gave him what was obviously a well-rehearsed pout. "You don't want anything?"

"I have an early day tomorrow." He kneeled on the mattress and leaned in so he could give her a deep, lingering kiss. "Need to go. You can stay. The room is paid for the night. I'll arrange for a taxi to take you home in the morning." He picked up his clothes from the floor and considered taking a shower. Maybe she'd join him. Fucking her against the cold marble wall would be enjoyable.

"So this is it? I won't see you again?"

He pulled on his slacks and hurried to button his shirt. He'd shower at home. Before jumping into bed with someone, Colin made sure to explain he wasn't looking for emotional entanglements. It was supposed to save both him and his occasional lover some time and drama, but there were always the ones who thought they could change him. Jules was apparently of that mind, so the sooner he was out of there, the better.

Tucking his shirt in his pants, he gave her a smile over his shoulder. "Never say never." It was better than trying to explain she was being unfair to him and to herself by expecting more than a one-time fling.

"I don't usually sleep with men I just met, you know," she called out when he opened the door to leave. He didn't break his stride.

He deleted her number from his contacts before he even reached the elevator.

Chapter Two

Colin turned the faucet most of the way to hot. He always liked his shower scalding. Hot water soothed him after a long day, and it had nothing to do with washing off the shame or whatever his idiot brother believed was wrong with him.

And that was because he felt no shame. He did nothing wrong.

He liked being surrounded by beauty, enveloped in it. He liked fucking it. A tight body was a fountain of youth. There was nothing more rejuvenating than watching a gorgeous model who ruled the runway crawl to him, asking to suck his cock. Brad called him superficial, and maybe Colin was, but beauty was a fragile, ephemeral thing, and he'd indulge in it for as long as he could. Which was why he'd never really go for someone like Becca, despite his momentary attraction to her during lunch.

He massaged soap down his torso and smiled. His pecs and abs were sculpted to perfection. Not an inch of flab. Not the body of a thirty-four year old realtor, but that of a twenty-something athlete.

Unlike his best friend, who was as white bread as they came, Colin was a social drinker and smoker, and occasionally partook in some recreational drug usage. His motto was, "If the pleasure is more than the pain, it's worth it." And he didn't mind a bit of pain anyway.

"Colin the Scoundrel." His voice reverberated off the glass walls of the stall and reached his ears muffled by the pelting water. He wasn't a scoundrel, despite what Becca called him. Despite what Brad had obviously told her. He didn't lie or take advantage of people. Never hid behind pretenses. He was down to fuck, and not interested in anything more.

It might not be what Brad or Becca deemed as nice, but he never hurt anyone — unless they explicitly asked for it and enjoyed it.

He liked what he liked, and he let his passions rule his life, but his choices had no repercussions on others. On the contrary. The degraded model swore she'd never come as hard as when he fucked her doggy style, her face pressed to the pillows. That was enough to make Colin come, even if she wasn't a spectacular lay. Many of them weren't, but the boost to his ego was a potent aphrodisiac.

He tried to soap his back, and for a moment regretted not taking that shower with Jules.

Who'd only given him her number because she thought she knew Becca.

Well, *he* wasn't the one who lied in this case.

He circled his limp cock with his thumb and finger, and pulled down on it, lathering its length and making it jump. It was his own touch, not the memory of Becca's hand disappearing under the table, that did that.

He conjured Jules's lithe body in his imagination. Thought of her going down on him. She was more skilled in the fantasy than she'd been in reality, when she only licked at his cockhead sloppily before he stopped her and took his turn eating her out until she begged for mercy.

He moved his hand faster on his hardening shaft, and Jules's greedy mouth gave its place to Brad's wide lips. Colin gritted his teeth. He shouldn't be doing this. If Brad ever found out Colin sometimes thought of him when he jerked off…

Colin pulled on himself faster, relishing the deliciously wrong mental image of his best friend kneeling naked before him.

Long, thick strings of cum shot from his dick and sprayed the glass. Dude. He'd already come once today; he hadn't expected to only last this little.

Or to have a flashback of Becca licking her lips, as his hips jerked one last time.

The water was still scorching when he quickly soaped up again. He rinsed and then used the showerhead to chase the last drops of his spendings down the drain.

The steam had fogged up the mirror, and Colin wiped enough of it clean with the hand towel that he could watch himself while he brushed his teeth and applied a thin layer of moisturizer. Other than a handful of smile lines around his eyes, and the two deeper grooves framing his mouth, his skin was smooth, and he intended for it to remain so.

He put on some deo and wrapped his bath towel around his hips. He had to call home, and that wasn't something he felt comfortable doing in the buff.

It was nice to know there were some lines he wouldn't cross.

He grabbed his cell phone and hopped on the couch, tightening the towel when it threatened to slip off.

He pressed 3, then *Call*.

"Hey, pumpkin." His mom was the only person to get away with calling him something so silly.

He didn't even bother to grouch about it. "Hey, Mom. How's Dad?"

"Annoying, but I'm not allowed to shoot him." She always gave a version of the same answer.

Colin chuckled anyway. "That's a relief."

"For you, maybe. I'm the one who keeps hearing how his leg hurts and how he hates being unable to scratch it. I had to pry one of my knitting needles away from him. He was trying to shove it inside his cast."

"Maybe next time he won't try to clean the rain gutters himself." Colin was glib about it now, but had been terrified when his mother called to say his father fell off the roof. He remembered rushing to the hospital and having it out with Alan, because he hadn't been there to help their father. Funny how Alan hadn't been there either, but he considered the accident to be Colin's fault.

Everything ever was Colin's fault. Because he went to college. Because he moved away. Because he made more money. Because he fucked men once in a while.

Memories of his brother's parting words made Colin's stomach churn. His jaw hurt, and the taste of copper made him wince. He'd bitten his tongue.

"...three more weeks."

"Sorry, Mom, missed that last part."

"I said I don't know how I'll survive your father's nagging for three more weeks. Maybe you should come down for a few days? Help me keep him in check? He's too much for just me and Alan." She gave a tight little laugh, but Colin heard the worry behind it. The hope her sons would patch things up.

"Can't take a leave now. Still fighting to prove I earned my place with the company."

"I understand."

He hated hearing her so sad. "Tell Alan I said hi."

"He said the same."

No, he hadn't, but Colin played along. He let his mother drag him into idle chit chat about things in Boston, and eventually used the same early-day-tomorrow excuse he'd given Jules, to get off the line.

He'd just poured himself a nightcap—solely to stop his tongue from bleeding, of course—when his cell rang.

Would people let him get some sleep?

The screen showed Brad's name under a funny picture from last year's Halloween party. He accepted the call and brought the phone to his ear. "What do you want, man? I'm about to turn in."

"Becca liked you," Brad said.

"Yeah? Tell her to get in line."

"Douche bag."

"Yup."

"So what do you think? About her?"

Colin thought his friend was too good looking for Becca and Becca was too sexual for Brad, but he shoved the impulse to say so aside. "You're right; she's fun. And smart." And Colin wanted to feel her boobs. *Shit.*

"She's all sorts of things. You should get to know her better." Pause. "I know. Movie, the three of us, tomorrow night."

Colin really had no reason to want to know her better, but he also had no excuse not to. If Becca was there to stay, he had to resolve his issues and accept her as his buddy's girlfriend. "Text me where and when, and I'll be there." He hastened to add, "But it better not be a chick flick."

Chapter Three

"Sorry I'm late. Broke a nail, and had to fix it."
Becca waggled her fingers at Brad, and smiled when he
clasped her wrist and kissed each fingertip. "Did you get
us tickets?"

"Got them." Colin waved them for her to see, and
took the time to really look at her. She wore skinny jeans.
He always believed skinny jeans were meant for skinny
women, but she more than pulled them off in her high
heels. Maybe it was the low-cut top that balanced it out.

And he was giving her too much thought.
Whatever made her look hot tonight wasn't his business.

Fuck. *Not* hot. Best friend's girl and all.

"See? You're more than eye candy." Becca swept
her gaze down his body and licked her lips, like she tasted
something scrumptious.

Colin shoved his hands in the pockets of his jacket
and wrapped it around him. The night wasn't that cold,
but he felt self-conscious under her scrutiny. "You ready
to go in?"

"Lead the way," Brad said.

Colin turned to do just that, but not before he saw
Brad cup Becca's ass. Couldn't he just keep his hands to
himself? It wasn't just the two of them outside the movie
theater. Some respect for other people wouldn't kill them.

Colin shook his head. Was he also going to tell those damned kids to get off his lawn? Brad was happily letting go of his hang-ups. Becca might not be the partner Colin envisioned for his best friend, but she made him happy. And that involved public displays of affection, whether Colin was comfortable with it or not. He'd get used to it.

Just not immediately.

Like, he might still feel uncomfortable when halfway through the rom-com they made him watch, he saw Becca trail her fingers up Brad's thigh and then not-so-subtly pop his fly.

Colin tried to return his attention to the movie, but it was hard. Like Brad's cock was, when Becca pulled it out and closed her fist around it. Colin wanted nothing more than to openly watch what took place next to him. Even in the darkened room, he could make out the drop of precum glistening on the red head of Brad's cock. Becca twisted her wrist, caught the drop on her thumb, and brought it to her mouth. She sucked it in slowly and then grasped Brad's shaft again and began pumping it.

Brad raised his hips to meet the movements of her hand. Maybe she wasn't good for him after all. She was making him completely forget he was Mr. Clean-Cut. He'd regret it when he came to his senses.

Colin faced the screen, but kept sliding his gaze to what Becca was doing. His mouth was dry. Beside him, Brad panted. Brad looked straight ahead, but when Colin chanced a more lingering look at his friend's face, he saw Brad's jaw was clenched, his eyes squeezed tight.

Colin was so hard, it hurt. Brad let a little moan slip out, and Colin found himself cupping his own cock over his jeans. Pressing down with the heel of his hand. He needed release too, and he envied Brad, who was about to get his.

But where? Was Becca going to make him spill on his pants, or would she stop and give Brad blue balls?

Just then, Becca ducked her head in Brad's lap. Brad didn't seem surprised at all, as if this was a regular occurrence, but Colin glanced around in panic. At least they were in the last row, so nobody seemed to notice the deviant—and no doubt illegal—behavior taking place right next to him.

When Becca sat back up, Colin realized he was staring. It didn't matter. They had to know he would see them. That he'd watch them.

Becca winked at him and rubbed her index finger along her bottom lip.

Brad elbowed him while trying to button up his jeans. "Sorry, man." Whether the apology was for the hand-and-mouth action or the jab in Colin's ribs, Brad's huge grin implied utter lack of remorse.

Colin's cock still throbbed when they left the cinema. He was going through a mental list of booty calls he could go for, when Brad suggested a night cap.

"Nah. I don't wanna be the third wheel," Colin said.

Brad and Becca exchanged a look, and then Becca said, "That doesn't have to be a bad thing."

Colin didn't know what the look meant, and he lacked the energy to find out. He shook his head. "I'll go home. Had a long day at the office. You crazy kids enjoy the rest of the night."

"If you're sure." Brad gave Colin the typical male half hug.

Becca, on the other hand, plastered her body to his. She smelled like wild flowers, and her breasts felt warm through his shirt. Colin had never touched breasts this big. The waifs he went for had small, firm tits that didn't jiggle when they walked. He wanted to zip up his jacket and shield himself against the warmth and the temptation.

Becca gave him a kiss on the corner of his lips. He thought she meant to go for the cheek, and he tried to turn his face more, but she moved with him.

"I hope you enjoyed it." She played with the short hair at the nape of his neck.

Surprise got the rest of his body as rigid as his cock. "The movie?" he asked in a whisper.

"Of course." She giggled and stepped back, hand already reaching for Brad's, fingers splayed. "We have to do this again, but next time you're coming for drinks too."

"I'll call you tomorrow, bro. May drop by." Brad tugged Becca after him, and the two crossed the street laughing.

Colin watched until they were swallowed by the crowd. Then he walked briskly to his car. The night had turned chillier, but a fire burned him up inside. He tried to cool off, but his thoughts kept returning to the couple that just left.

They seemed so happy together, and Becca appeared completely in love with Brad.

So why did Colin have the feeling she was coming on to him?

He got in the driver's seat, turned on the ignition, and raked his fingers through his short cropped hair. Should he say something to Brad?

He peeled off without checking the side-view mirror, and barely missed a passing car. A horn blared, but Colin was preoccupied. *What* could he say, when he just had a vague suspicion? He'd only seen Becca twice in as many days. He didn't know her. She didn't have a shy bone in her body, but that didn't mean she'd hit on her boyfriend's best friend. And Brad wasn't an idiot. If he didn't mind her overt sexuality, why should Colin?

In fact, Colin shouldn't give her another thought. He should call Liv and get lost between her mile-long legs for the night. Liv, who never turned him down and was up for anything. Eyes on the road, he pulled out his phone, pressed the voice-command key, and said, "Liv."

"Do you want to call Liv?" the nasal electronic voice asked.

He began to say yes, but it was almost eleven, and he had to be at the office in the morning.

And Liv tended to be boring when her ankles weren't framing her ears. She never got his jokes and was always on about one diet or another.

"Screw it," he said.

"Command not recognized. Please try again."

He tossed the phone on the passenger seat and drove the rest of the way home, trying hard not to think of women he shouldn't be thinking of. Women he didn't find attractive anyway.

His phone rang a couple hours later, but he was busy pulling on his cock. In the morning he saw he had a missed call and text from Brad.

The text read, "If you liked how it looked, you should see how it feels."

Colin started his day with another wank.

By the time he got to work, he'd decided Brad and Becca were messing with him. Maybe it was a loyalty test. Brad wanted to see what kind of friend he was, and if he'd take advantage of the openings—ha—Becca gave him. Or they could be trying to teach him a lesson? Show him big girls had moves too?

That was mean. Becca wasn't big. She was curvy. Though he typically considered anyone not in possession of a flat stomach overweight.

Okay, lesson learned. He might not be into her, but he admitted Becca was attractive. Not to him. In general.

He pinched the bridge of his nose and crashed his thumb on the intercom button. "Simon. Coffee. And two aspirin."

"Rough night, Mr. D?" His assistant sounded as cheeky as always. It was one of the reasons Colin had hired him, the others being his great ass and quick wit—in that order. Now his cheekiness added to the pressure building behind Colin's eyes.

Colin let go of the button. Yelling would get him nowhere. Simon knew his value and wasn't intimidated by even the foulest of Colin's moods.

The proof was in Simon's smile, when he brought the coffee and pills. "Maybe a massage will help?"

Would it ever? Simon had long, pianist fingers and a mouth that seemed made for sucking cock. Unfortunately, an interoffice affair was on the short list of lines Colin wouldn't cross. "Just the aspirin, thanks." He kept his tone professional, but couldn't help a grin at the dramatic roll of Simon's eyes.

"Well, if you change your mind, you know where I'll be," Simon said on his way out.

Another look-but-not-touch situation. Colin seemed surrounded by those lately.

He leaned back against the headrest and closed his eyes. He couldn't think that way. He didn't seriously consider doing something with Simon, and couldn't possibly be attracted to Becca. Even if Brad wasn't falling for her—maybe already in love with her?—she didn't meet Colin's specifications. Some liked blondes, some liked brunettes, and he liked lean, perfect bodies. Simple as that.

Maybe he was getting older and yearned for something that lasted longer than a night or two. A relationship like Brad's, with someone who shared his interests and sense of humor, and who was a tiger in the sack, like Colin bet Becca was.

Someone more to his taste, naturally. But maybe with boobs like Becca's.

He wondered what her nipples looked like. They were responsive, for sure. The evening breeze had made them stretch the fabric of her blouse. He loved women's nipples. Loved their rubbery feel on his lips and tongue. Loved feeling them harden against his palms.

Becca's breasts looked heavy. They'd fill his hands. Her nipples would be a dusky pink, with large areolas.

Fuck.

He thumped his head repeatedly with the heel of his hand. No, no, no, no. Such thoughts were wrong. Next he'd start wondering if she trimmed or waxed—

"Fuck."

He had to call Brad. Tell him they had to set some boundaries. That he didn't like watching Becca jerk him off.

Then why had he watched?

That Becca pressing herself to him made him feel weird.

That she got him hard.

He had to say something. If it was a test, he'd pass. If it wasn't… he didn't care. He'd still act as a good friend should, and then he'd go out and fuck someone who could be on the cover of Vogue, and forget all about the curvy brunette.

Or he'd just avoid Brad and Becca all together, until being near them felt safe again.

Chapter Four

"You free for lunch?"

Colin only briefly looked up from his paperwork. "No, I'm not. As I already told you when you called me, fifteen minutes ago." He wasn't really that busy, but he had enough on his plate he didn't feel bad using work as an excuse not to meet up with Brad and Becca.

"Come on, man. You've been avoiding me for days. And you have to eat." Brad rarely took no for an answer. Colin's inner salesman usually found that admirable, but today it annoyed him.

"I've been busy. We can do drinks tonight." He glanced at his phone. "Have to finish this up, and then I'm showing a couple that two-story in Richmond district at four. Should be done by six, so wanna meet somewhere at eight?" That gave him enough time to come up with an excuse to cancel.

"We didn't mean to make you uncomfortable. At the cinema. We thought you'd be cooler about it."

Cooler? While Brad got a blowjob right next to him? Colin fought hard to refrain from looking up at Brad. "I don't know what you mean." But his heart sped up at the memory.

"I want you to have sex with Becca."

"What?" The pen fell from Colin's hand and rolled off his desk. He ducked after it. "I don't think I heard you right." He couldn't have. And he had no idea why he was sporting a semi.

"Come out from under there."

Colin sat up, pen in hand. "Okay, say again."

"I want you to have sex with Becca," Brad said again.

So he *had* heard right. And he'd been spot on about the reason behind the other night's exhibition. Relief and anger made his gut roil. "Is this some elaborate scheme to test her loyalty? Or mine? Are you asking me to do it, just to see if I will?" And could Colin please convince himself that he never would?

Brad shook his head. "What's with the conspiracy theories? You're not right in the head, you know."

"And yet I'm not the one asking my best friend to fuck my girlfriend." Colin must have raised his voice, because his assistant's head popped at the opening of his office door.

"Everything all right, Mr. D?"

"Yeah, Simon. Thanks." Colin stood and shut the door, then leaned against it. "Brad, can you please explain what got into you? You and Becca seemed fine at the movies. I've never seen you more taken with a woman, and now you want me to… what? Take her off your hands?"

"It's not like that. I'll be there too." Brad sighed. "It's her thirtieth birthday next Saturday. I asked if she wanted something special, and she said a threesome. Two men and her."

"She asked for me?" Colin was lightheaded. He needed to sit down. Becca wanted to sleep with him, and Brad was okay with that. More. He'd join them. Christmas had come early this year.

But he shouldn't unwrap his fucking presents, because it wasn't fucking right.

He forced his feet to move and dropped his weight on the leather couch.

"I suggested you." Brad straddled the armrest, no longer looking at him.

Colin loosened his tie. It was getting too hot. "So you thought of me?"

"Who else, man? You know I don't… I'm not very open with sex, and you're as experienced as they get. No offence."

"None taken," mumbled Colin.

"I wanted to ease you into it, but you've disappeared for the past couple of weeks. When Becca and I got together, she told me she likes to spice things up on occasion, and I promised to try anything once." He shrugged. "You and I won't be doing anything *together*, but I'd still rather have you there than some random guy I'll have to pay. It'll be less awkward."

Colin didn't see how that was possible. In the early days of their friendship, he'd let Brad know he occasionally indulged in some male company of the naked variety, but he hadn't been completely honest with him. When Colin first offered to buy Brad a drink, he meant to seduce the tall, dark, and handsome momma's boy. Colin forgot all about his plans when he and Brad found themselves geeking over Farscape, and he never regretted it. He wouldn't trade his friendship with Brad for a single night of passion, however hot that night might be.

But now Colin could have it all. He could be in bed with Brad. He could fuck the same woman as him—a woman he found inexplicably alluring. And it would all be consequence free.

Of course, if he were a true friend, he'd let Brad know there was still this one parameter Brad wasn't aware of. Two, counting in Colin's possible attraction to Becca.

Nah, he wouldn't do it. Too messy. Too complicated.

"Just think about it, will you?" Brad stood and turned to face him. "Maybe go out with us a couple more times? You could talk to Becca alone too. See exactly what she has in mind."

Colin pulled a cushion in his lap and thumbed its zipper, nodding mutely. He hoped he looked nonchalant and that Brad wouldn't realize he was trying to hide his erection.

"So it's not an outright no. Yes?" Brad backed toward the door.

"I'll think about it, but it's not a good idea."

"I'll come over tonight. Maybe bring Becca. We can have a drink. Talk about it all."

Before Colin had time to come up with an answer, Brad was gone, the door closed behind him.

* * * *

Colin kicked off his shoes, grabbed a beer from the fridge, and hopped onto his leather sofa. He downed a swig of the beer and loosened his tie. The remote in hand, he flicked on the television and tried hard to find something to watch. Anything to take his mind off Brad's offer. His workday had been busy, but now he was home, insidious thoughts kept creeping into his conscience.

He said he'd think about the possibility of a threesome, but he obviously had to say no. Neither relationships nor friendships came back from something like that.

Unless it was done right.

No. There was no 'doing it right' when it came to fucking your friend's girl. Especially at the same time said friend was fucking her.

Would Brad want to go in the front or back? What would Colin prefer?

He remembered Becca's round ass, swaying as she walked. After all those years chasing perfect bodies, he might not mind hitting that, to be honest.

But he couldn't possibly be honest, if he wanted things to remain as they were.

'If' being the operative word.

He guzzled down the rest of his beer, stood, and slipped off his tie. On his way to the kitchen, he peeled off his shirt and draped it over one of the dining room chairs. He'd have one more beer and then jump in the shower. Brad hadn't called. He probably had second thoughts, which meant Colin could let the whole thing go.

He was halfway through the second bottle, when the downstairs doorbell rang.

Colin neared the intercom and pressed the button. "Who is it?"

"It's us." This was Brad's voice, and *us* could only mean him and Becca. In Colin's building. While Colin was on his way to getting drunk. Someone up there sure loved putting his defenses to the test.

He couldn't pretend he wasn't in. He could say he had company, but Brad might want details the next day, and Colin wasn't used to lying. Not to his friends, at least.

He slammed his palm on the wall. "Come on up." He buzzed them in and hurried to put his shirt back on, before getting the upstairs door.

When Becca walked out of the elevator, Colin knew she was determined to get him to say yes. Her low-cut ruched dress hugged her curves, its deep red color bringing out the green flecks in her eyes. She'd piled her hair atop her head in a messy bun that left tendrils caressing her face, and her high heels made her legs look long and shapely.

"Do I pass inspection?" she asked.

If Colin were any less jaded, he might have blushed. "I'm sorry, who are you?" he asked with a smile. "I've only met Brad's other girlfriend, the house painter. You know, kind of scruffy?"

Brad wrapped a possessive arm around her waist and kissed the exposed nape of her neck. "Doesn't she look gorgeous?"

Colin hated to admit it, but she did. Brad had been right. Becca was sexy. And unless Colin reined himself in, both she and Brad would be able to tell Colin wanted her.

Shit. He actually wanted her. There was no denying it any longer.

"She got all dressed up for you," Brad said. "Maybe I should be jealous."

"Quit that." Colin arched an eyebrow at Brad and then turned to her. "Wine?"

"I'd rather have a beer." She nodded toward his empty bottles.

"Make that two," said Brad.

Even better. The short trip to the kitchen would give Colin time to gather himself. He grabbed two bottles of Samuel Adams from the bridge and called out, "You need a glass, Becca?" He knew Brad didn't.

"No." Her voice came from right behind him. When he turned his head, she was a hairsbreadth away. "We're going to need more than two. Let me help you." She reached past him, pressing her breasts against his side, and grabbed another couple of bottles.

She hopped on the bench and used her thumb ring to pop one bottle open. Colin watched as she wrapped her lips around the opening and drank greedily. When she extended her tongue to lick a drop that slowly glided down the neck of the bottle, he had to bite back a groan at the memory of the last time he saw her mouth at work. She *really* knew how to use it.

Becca arched an eyebrow. "Brad told me he asked you."

The words took a heartbeat to register. "I don't—"

"Please say yes. It will mean a lot to both of us." She ran her tongue along her upper lip. "I'll make it worth your while."

He had to look away. "Becca... I don't think it's a good idea." A specific part of him disagreed strongly with that statement, but he had to listen to his upper head for once.

"Is it because I'm not a model?" She cocked her head. She might have sounded insecure, if it weren't for the mischief lighting up her eyes.

No. Yes. She wasn't his type, but that wasn't the only factor. There was nothing to gain by insulting her, when his main reason was so noble. He shook his head. "Having sex with you will ruin my friendship with Brad and probably mess up your relationship with him. He may act cool, but he's not ready to share you. I don't know if he ever will be."

She gave him a slow, lazy smile. "You'd be surprised at what he's ready for."

He wanted to ask and milk her answer for all the details he could get from this voluptuous woman.

Voluptuous?

No. He didn't think of her as voluptuous. She didn't have what he looked for in a woman. He had to keep reminding himself that, since thinking he wouldn't sleep with a friend's girlfriend didn't seem to do the trick. Becca was at least twenty pounds overweight. Maybe even thirty. She was round where she should be flat, curvy where she should be toned, and her breasts were several cups larger than the perfect, fit-in-a-champagne-glass, size.

His gaze traveled to the swell of her cleavage, and he found himself thinking of her nipples again.

Utterly fucked-up train of thought.

"Why me?" He hadn't meant for the question to sound so husky.

She looked at him, as if the answer should have been obvious. "Because I want you, and Brad said I can have you." She trailed a nail down his cheek. "If a threesome is too much, I can ask him if we can be alone."

That was a weird thing to say. She and Brad were already—

"Oh." Realization sank in. "You mean you and me?"

"Yes."

He was short of breath at the thought of her taking his cock into her mouth. He gulped. "He won't like it." Why was he turning it on Brad? Colin was the one who shouldn't like it.

Becca gave him another of those mysterious smiles. "He'll agree, if I promise to make it worth his while."

"You shouldn't even ask him. He'll hate me for telling you, but I think he's falling for you. Hard. He'll probably agree to anything that will make you happy, and then resent you for it. He'll resent us both. This can't end well, Becca."

She slid down from her perch, letting her dress ride high on her thighs. They were creamy white and fleshy. Biteable.

He was supposed to be thinking of croissants that way, not Becca.

She lifted his chin with a finger and brushed his ear with her lips. "On the contrary, I foresee a happy ending for all of us."

Colin suppressed the entirely pleasurable shiver that travelled down his spine, and waited until she was out of the kitchen to splash some cold water on his face.

It all sounded *good*, when it clearly shouldn't. Even if a threesome or a night of debauchery — in whatever combination — was appealing, Becca shouldn't be getting him hard. She wasn't even close to the level of pussy he was used to.

But he bet she was amazing in bed. Or on the kitchen counter.

"…the fuck?" He shook his head and ran his palm down his face, chasing the mental picture away. He'd never find out for sure if she was the greatest fuck in the world, *because she was fucking Brad's fucking girlfriend.* He shouldn't be considering touching her, but from what he'd seen, there was no way he could give her that argument and win. He had to talk to Brad instead.

If those two were set on spicing up their sex life, they could turn to a pro. Colin would be no part of it.

He waited until his heartbeat was mostly back to normal, then grabbed a pack of chips from the counter and tucked two more bottles of beer under his arm. "Anyone up for Scrabble?" he asked, as he reentered the living room. He might survive the night, if he kept things friendly and nerdy.

Or maybe there was no salvation for him, because he had a filthy mind and a wandering eye.

Even though Becca and Brad were obviously dressed for a night out, they both agreed to play, and neither of them went with the juvenile option of going for four letter words, as Colin initially expected. Still, he couldn't help but stare at how Becca's breasts jiggled when she bounced in place after turning 'phone' into 'xylophone.' And his gaze kept returning to the apex of her thighs, as her dress rode higher with every exuberant motion.

She couldn't possibly be aware of how much she was turning him on.

No. It wasn't her turning him on. Couldn't be. What got him hard was the idea of the forbidden fruit. Better yet, the idea of a three-way with a guy on whom Colin had long given up.

Becca leaned forward, attention focused solely on the board in front of her. Her legs slid open just an inch. Colin couldn't really see anything — her dress and the dim lighting hid the triangle that gave him such a headache — but he imagined he could. In his mind's eye, he saw nothing but glistening bare flesh, and he was close enough to run his fingers along her slit. Kneeling in front of her. Tasting her.

He realized he was staring and snapped his gaze to her face. Her brow was furrowed in concentration, but the corners of her lips twisted slightly, as she opened her knees another fraction.

Panic rising inside him, Colin threw a glance at Brad, who appeared absorbed sorting out a word for his turn to play. Should he keep looking?

Most certainly not. It wasn't like there was anything between her legs he hadn't seen before. At the end of the day, wasn't all pussy just pussy?

Becca tapped a tile on the coffee table rhythmically, the letter hidden from view. The fingers of her free hand glided up her inner thigh, blood red fingernails drawing circles on the creamy skin.

She knew he was watching.

Of course she knew.

This time, when she leaned forward to form the word 'COME,' she spread her legs wide for just one moment—long enough for him to catch a glimpse of what might have been nude panties.

Or not.

He shook his head and didn't miss the wide smile on Becca's full lips. She knew, and she loved every reaction he had.

But Colin wasn't born yesterday, and he certainly wasn't a sex-starved kid. Once he reminded himself that, focusing on the game became infinitely easier. Becca wasn't the first woman who tried to seduce him. She wouldn't be the first to fail, either. Fuck, he'd turned down gorgeous, willowy creatures, because he didn't like something as insignificant as their pedicure. He loved being shallow. He was good at it. He wouldn't let her and her curves and her mind-games get to him.

Even if her pout was the sexiest pout he'd seen on a woman.

He closed his eyes and faked a yawn. He wasn't ruled by his dick, damn it.

His dick probably laughed at him.

Chapter Five

Scrabble failed to keep their interest after the third round of beers, and Colin hoped folding up the board would signify the end of the evening.

Brad apparently had other ideas. "Anyone up for a movie? I'd watch something." Doubtful. His eyelids seemed heavy. Maybe he was hoping for a repeat of their night at the movies.

"I can see what's on TV," Colin said. With any luck, there'd be nothing on, and they'd leave him alone.

Becca gave him a half-smile and stood. "I'll grab another beer. Let's see if you can find an oldie. I don't feel like action tonight."

And thank fuck for that, if she meant it the way Colin understood.

Brad shrugged. "I'm good with anything you decide."

Colin kept flicking through channels, his attention more on how Brad kicked off his shoes and propped his legs on the couch, than on the screen. Now there was no room for Becca to sit on that couch.

"Oh, wait. It's Battlestar Galactica." Becca bounced in the living room, waving at the TV. "Go back. Go back."

Colin did just that. "Huh. It's the original series." He pressed the info button. "And it's apparently a marathon."

"Never saw it," Brad said. He yawned and crossed his arms on his stomach.

"Starbuck was a guy in this one," Becca said, gaining another ounce of Colin's respect.

"What a waste." Brad laughed.

"I know, right?" Becca toed off her own shoes, sat next to Colin, and folded her legs beneath her.

Great. Now she was close enough to touch. He needed an excuse to move to the armchair before she made a move.

Only the show finished, Brad started snoring gently, and Becca barely looked at him.

Colin felt compelled to say something. "Brad is asleep." Well, that sounded like an invitation, when it so clearly wasn't.

Was it?

Becca nodded. "Mind if I stay for one more episode? My dad and I used to watch it when I was little, and it still has some of its old magic. I know the special effects are stupid and the dialog is cheesy, but…" She bit her lip. "Unless you need to go to bed." It seemed to be an unconscious gesture, but it was as flirty as anything she'd done. She flirted even when she wasn't trying, and Colin was fighting a lost battle.

"I can stay up for one more. You okay for drinks?" He tilted his head toward her empty bottle.

"I better not have more. I'll probably have to drive us back. Doubt Brad will be up to it."

Colin nodded. "You could crash here." What the fuck was he saying? "I mean, I have two couches."

Smile lines formed at the corners of her eyes. "Thanks. We'll see how we are after this. Now hush. It's starting."

Colin hushed, but didn't watch the show. Instead, he watched Becca absorb every single moment of it, commenting gleefully on things she remembered from the first time she saw it. She seemed so innocent. So open. No trace remained of the seductress who'd walked into his apartment.

And somehow that seduced him even more.

Two hours later, Becca cracked her knuckles, arched her back, and rolled her head. "Can't believe we've watched two episodes back to back, and I'm still not sleepy." Her eyelids drooped, but Colin didn't burst her bubble. "Shouldn't you go to bed?" she asked. "Just help me wake Brad, and we'll be out of here."

"I'm not sleepy either. Let's watch one more." He couldn't care less about Battlestar Galactica at this point. Becca had let down her hair, literally and figuratively. Her curls framed her face, and Colin wanted to wrap a ringlet around his finger and see if it felt as silky as it looked.

"Okay, but my back hurts. I need to get more comfy." She squished a throw pillow between her hands, scrunched her nose, and then looked at him. "This isn't a come-on. I'm too tired for sex now anyway."

Before Colin could get past his incredulity and ask what she meant, Becca stretched out on her side and laid her head in his lap.

"Ah, that's better," she said.

Not for him. Now she was inches from his cock. And what was he supposed to do with his hand? He closed it into a fist. Spread his arm out and propped it along the back of the couch. Not exactly comfortable.

In the end, he placed it on her shoulder. If he just rested it there and didn't move, he could pretend it wasn't her flawless skin burning his fingertips. And maybe he would stop wanting to ghost his palm along the line of her cleavage and cup the breasts drawing his gaze with every breath she took.

She tossed back her hair, and a single tendril glided along the back of his hand. He moved fast and trapped it under his thumb. It did feel like silk, and he knew it smelled deliciously.

Why had he asked her to stay? To prolong his agony?

He didn't know what agony meant, until she slid one hand under his thigh. Colin squirmed, expecting her touch to become bolder. It didn't, but her fingers seared him through the denim.

"I thought this wasn't a come-on," he managed through gritted teeth.

"Huh?" She looked up at him, and he saw real confusion in her eyes.

"Nothing. I'm seeing things." And she'd soon be feeling them, if he didn't calm down.

"Must be the hour." She smiled. Except for a thin red outline, her lipstick had faded to a faint pink stain. Her mascara was smudged under her right eye, and her right cheek bore a red mark from where it pressed against his leg.

She was beautiful.

He had to say something. Something to make her stop looking at him, because if she didn't turn those hazel eyes away, he'd pull her to him and kiss her breathless.

"So you liked Starbuck more as a girl?" He tugged lightly on her hair and nodded toward the television.

Becca got comfortable again. "I'd totally do her."

He gulped. This wasn't exactly helping him calm down. He'd have to try a different subject. "Your dad — you seemed sad when you said he watched it with you. Is he… gone?"

She didn't seem surprised by his question. "No, he's still around, and he and my mother are still happily married. We're just not that close anymore."

"Yeah, time has a way of doing that to people."

"So do unfulfilled expectations." She drew a circle on his knee with her free hand.

Yeah, he knew about those too. "Who let whom down?" He read the answer in the tightening of her shoulders, but she confirmed it.

"I did. I wasn't the perfect daughter he wanted me to be. Or maybe the perfect son he never had. Didn't get into sports. Was way too interested in boys. Not interested enough in being told what to do." She chuckled, but it sounded forced. "We've had our ups and downs, and when I was seventeen, he kicked me out of the house for six weeks, so I'd get over my wild ways. I've been on my own since I finished college, and that I put aside my degree in order to paint houses made matters worse. But we eventually reached a silent agreement. I keep my personal life away from him, and we play house once a month, when he and Mom have me over for dinner."

She spoke in a detached, emotionless tone. A tone he'd used more than once, to explain why he and his older brother weren't hanging out any more, even before their final fallout. A tone someone practiced because they didn't want outsiders to see their pain. But he saw. He saw her. And she was fucking incredible.

"You're wrong." He had to whisper the words, because of the catch in his throat.

She rubbed her eyes and sat up to look at him. "What?" She looked so vulnerable. So fragile.

"You're wrong. You didn't let them down. They did. They should be nothing but proud of the strong, independent, beautiful woman you are. Instead, they made you doubt yourself."

Her eyes brimmed with unshed tears, but her smile was dazzling. "Is this a line? Because I meant it when I said I was too tired for sex."

He'd done this too—joke when all he wanted to do was crawl somewhere dark and lick his wounds. Still, he'd respect her choice and play along. "Come on. Not even a blow job?" He waggled his eyebrows.

She let out some kind of surprised giggle-snort. "You're terrible."

"But I made you laugh." And the fact that it made his heart constrict in his chest meant more than he was willing to process.

"You did." She locked her gaze to his, and he felt naked. Exposed.

He caught himself leaning toward her, closing the distance between them until their faces were only a couple of inches apart. Becca licked her lips, and Colin sucked in a breath. He had to escape her magnetic field, before he crashed and burned.

He straightened his body. "Let me get you covers and a pillow. There's no way Brad is waking up. Listen to him snore."

Becca nodded. "I'd appreciate a pair of sweatpants and a Tee, if you can spare them."

"Sure." Anything to get away from her for a couple minutes, to catch his breath and put his thoughts in order.

He returned and handed her the bedding and clothes. "I'll leave you to get changed."

"Who hurt you?"

The question hit him so hard, his ears buzzed. He dropped more than sat on the arm of the couch. "I'm sorry, I don't—"

"You recognized my pain, because you've felt it. Who made you feel small and insufficient?"

He shook his head. "I don't want to talk about it now. It's late. We should sleep."

She looked at him a moment longer, then gave a little shrug. "You'll tell me sooner or later. It'll be good for you to share." She waved him off, turned her back to him, and lifted the hem of her dress. "Go. Sleep. Goodnight."

He mumbled, "Goodnight," and hurried to the safety of his room. Even closing and locking his bedroom door didn't make him safe from his thoughts, though. This night had changed things. Made them clear. Made it impossible for him to deny his attraction to her any longer.

Which only meant one thing—he should never be alone with her again.

If he was, he couldn't be held accountable for what happened.

Chapter Six

"Mr. Daniels?" Simon opened the door without knocking. "Mr. Miller is here for you. Again." The hint of a smile on Simon's face indicated he believed there was something naughty behind Brad's consecutive visits. He wasn't entirely wrong.

Brad bypassed Colin's assistant, pushed the door all the way open, and waltzed right in, as if he owned the place. "Told him you'd see me."

"It's okay, Simon," Colin said. "Go get us a couple iced mocha lattes and two bagels with lox, from that place I like." That place was on the other side of downtown San Francisco, and Simon's trek there and back would afford Colin and Brad some privacy.

"Sure thing, boss."

"Thanks for last night," Brad said, once there were no prying ears around. "Becca said you were the one who insisted we stay over."

Had Becca told him about their conversation too? How close they'd been to kissing?

"I just wish I'd been awake." Brad gave Colin a grin too cheeky for a straight male to be gracing his best friend with.

Colin maintained his calm despite Brad's sexy dimples. "No problem. You could have thanked me over the phone, though."

"Yeah, but I need a favor and thought I'd ask up close."

"I still haven't agreed to the last one." Colin snorted. "You sure are a demanding little bitch lately, huh?"

Brad chuckled. "This one is going to make you some money, so I'd hear me out, if I were you." He made himself at home on Colin's couch and propped a loafered foot on Colin's lacquered table.

"For the last time—I'm not a gigolo." Colin kept his voice light, but he resented the implication money would override his concern for their friendship. Especially after how hard he tried to be good the night before.

"I'm still not sold on that, but this is something entirely different. My mother needs you to move a property for her."

"And you couldn't call to tell me that?"

"Eh, there's a lovely little bistro right around the corner from the apartment. Thought we'd do lunch. And maybe talk?"

"About your crazy-ass idea again?" And how crazy was Colin for not finding it so preposterous any longer?

"If that's what you want."

"Fuck off, Brad."

"That's what I'm trying to do, dude, and you're throwing a wrench in it."

Colin shook his head. "Let me make some calls and tell Simon we don't need those coffees after all, and then we can head out."

"I'm driving."

"Knock yourself out."

* * * *

The place was within walking distance of the western side of Golden Gate Park, and the bistro was indeed lovely. Small, dimly lit, and quiet, it was a pleasant break from the frantic lunchtime atmosphere of most places Colin chose for a quick bite.

The discussion topic was less relaxing.

"Have you given it some thought? Becca's birthday present?"

Had he done anything but? "Yeah, and I still think it's a lousy idea."

"Why? We're three adults making informed choices." Brad's voice was quiet. Conversational. He wasn't disagreeing, his tone said. He just wanted to understand. Colin knew it was a trick Brad learned in law school, before he gave up law to manage his mother's construction company. "Nobody's getting hurt," Brad said, "and God knows you've been part of a threesome before."

He had. He'd been on one end of several, as well as smack dab in the middle of a couple. Hell, he participated in a full-blown celebratory orgy, when he first bought half of D&M Realty.

But he hadn't cared about any of the other participants, and he cared about Brad. "You two have been together for a very short time. Are you sure your relationship can take this? Shit, screw your relationship with Becca. You've only known her for five minutes. Are you sure you won't resent *me* when you see me balls deep in your woman?"

Brad cringed. Colin didn't know if it was because of the visual or his crudeness, but he went with it. "See? You can't even deal with the thought."

"I can't deal with the old lady behind you hearing what's spewing from your mouth."

"Hey. It's not— You're the one who wants to do this."

"That doesn't mean I want the whole establishment to know."

"All right." Colin lowered his voice to a whisper. "You want me to fuck your girlfriend, while you're inside her too. You want me pounding her pussy, while your cock is inside her ass." Fuck, he was turning himself on, but he had to make sure Brad got the entire picture. "But are you sure you're cool with us locking gazes over her shoulder, while we thrust inside her? Or are you going to keep your eyes shut the entire time? You've never done this before. I have. I've felt another guy's cock rub against my own. Do you know what that's like? Do you realize our balls may slap together?

"You said we wouldn't be doing anything to each other, but we'll both be there, Brad. Naked. Inside the same woman. *Your* girlfriend. Are you sure you can deal with every aspect of this?"

Brad was flushed, his tanned skin turned almost crimson on his cheeks. He was clearly uncomfortable, but was he convinced?

Colin narrowed his eyes, waiting for a response that took too long coming. "Well?" he asked.

Brad splayed long fingers on the table, framing the enormous bowl of Cobb salad in front of him. "You're right," he said, and for a moment Colin teetered between relief and disappointment. His buddy had seen the light.

"You're right," Brad said again. "I haven't done this before, but I want to. I've thought of everything you just mentioned, talked about it all with Becca, and we both want to. If being with us freaks you out, I can understand and accept it. Your choice to make. But it's not your responsibility to protect my relationship with her, and I doubt it says much about our friendship, if you think I'd risk it for one night of fun. I wouldn't ask you for this, if I thought it would drive a wedge between us, but if you can't handle it, we'll forget we ever had this discussion."

Colin was speechless. This assertive side of Brad was one he'd never seen before. And he liked it.

Oh, fuck.

Why was he hesitating? All he needed to do was tell Brad he wasn't into having sex with the both of them—that he wasn't into Becca—and the subject would be closed.

"Well?" Brad arched an eyebrow. He seemed cool as a cucumber now, and Colin felt his own temperature rising.

He was in control. He had to remember he was in control, no matter how messed up the situation was. He sucked in his lower lip and motioned for the waitress. "I'll have another glass of red," he said when she approached.

Brad folded his arms over his impressive chest. "So we're going with the, never-had-this-convo option?"

"Shut up."

"I mean, I get it, but Becca will be upset. She was really looking forward to it."

Colin's wine came, and he guzzled half of it down before speaking again. "I told her I wasn't crazy about the idea." He wanted to know how much of the previous night Becca had shared with Brad. If she'd kept her offer for a… one-on-one prelude to the main thing from him, Colin would put a final end to things then and there.

"And she told me she proposed a way for you to get more comfortable with it."

"She did." His cock, still half hard from earlier, stirred at the memory of her in his kitchen, suggesting the two of them had sex first.

"And you—"

"I said you wouldn't go for it."

"Like you said I would ultimately regret sharing her with you."

"Exactly."

Brad smirked.

"What?"

"Nothing." He produced his phone and typed something before slipping it back into his suit jacket that hung on the back of his chair. "You having anything else? I need to pop by the office for a few."

"Nah, I'm okay, but aren't we seeing the apartment?" Colin asked for the bill and handed the waitress his credit card.

"Shit. Yeah…" Brad tossed a set of keys on the table, already getting up to leave. "You go right up. Third floor, second to last apartment on your left. Check it out, and I'll be back in an hour or so, tops."

"Or we could come back tomorrow?"

"No, no. You go. I'll catch up."

Chapter Seven

Colin took the stairs up, wanting to see the condition the building was in. Mint didn't begin to cover it. The interior appeared to have been renovated quite recently, and if it was Brad's construction company who undertook it, they had to have a new crew. New painters, at least. The coating was flawless.

He didn't even pant—thank you, three hours a week at the gym—but by the time he hit the third floor landing, he was breaking a light sweat. He should have taken off his jacket before the climb.

He did just that outside the apartment, and folded the jacket over his arm before pushing the key into the lock. It only took a half turn for him to open the door. Made sense that the place wasn't locked up. What could someone steal from an empty property?

He toed the door open and looked at the floor. Hardwood and unmarked. Excellent. The smell of fresh paint greeted him as he passed the threshold, and he made sure to keep clear from the pale yellow walls. He generally disliked yellow anything, but in this case they infused the light that entered the large windowpanes with a warm glow. The place would be bright till late in the afternoon. He was giddy with excitement over handling the case on Mrs. Miller's behalf. This beauty would earn him a hefty commission that could buy him some time away from the city.

"Brad? Is that you?" Becca's voice reached him from the other room, and every muscle in his body tightened. He wasn't ready to see her. The previous night had shifted something inside him, and until he knew how to change things back, he had to keep his distance.

He held his breath for a heartbeat and closed the distance to the window to look outside. Location was a big selling point in his profession. He could move property overlooking a sewer, if he spun it the right way, but the unobstructed view to Golden Gate Bridge would sell itself.

Also, if he pretended not to hear her, maybe she'd stop calling.

"Brad?" The voice was closer now.

"No. It's me." His breath fogged the glass. He squeezed his eyes shut for a minute, until he finally gathered the courage to turn and face her.

The view inside the apartment was as curvy and magnificent as the scenery outside. Becca's hair was in a tight bun, but the rest of her appearance didn't share the severity of her up do. A loose, faded blue T-shirt hung low on one shoulder and reached down to the middle of her thighs. It looked like she wore nothing underneath. Colin's gaze zeroed in on the hot pink bra strap visible. The color looked striking against the pallor of her skin. Maybe he could focus on that, instead of the trickle of sweat gliding down her neck and disappearing between her breasts.

"You need something?" she asked. Her voice was throaty. It scratched down his back like he wanted her nails to.

Fuck. He had to stop wanting her. "Brad said I should come up and see the place. Didn't realize you'd be here."

"I wanted to do the bedroom before I left. Want to watch?" There was nothing innocent about the way she asked the question.

Colin found himself following her down a short corridor and through a door to his right. The room they entered was as large as his living room, but that wasn't what gave him pause. Unlike the living room that was unfurnished, the bedroom held a king-size mattress smack dab in the middle of the floor. And the ceiling was mirrored.

He pulled at his lower lip. This wasn't good. Not good at all. All he could think of was pushing Becca face-first onto the mattress and finding out what was under her shirt.

"There's a mattress on the floor." He had a special knack for stating the obvious.

Becca didn't laugh at him. "There's also a fridge in the kitchen, stocked with beer. Want one?"

He shook his head, gaze to the ceiling. "Just water, if you have any." Could he see down her front from this angle? He rubbed his face with both hands. A drink was the last thing he needed; he was already losing his grip, and alcohol would push him over the edge.

"Is tap okay?" she asked?

"Sure."

She left, and retuned with a bottle of beer and a plastic cup filled with water.

Colin was surprised his hand was steady when he reached for the drink. "Thank you." He downed his water in a few gulps and threw the empty cup in a plastic trash bag that lay by the door. "Brad should be here shortly. I can wait for him outside. I don't want to keep you from your work."

"You're not." She sunk to the mattress and crossed her legs, knees wide apart.

Colin had a hard time not staring at the exposed flesh, and let out a small sigh of relief when he made out the hemline of a pair of denim shorts.

"With what Brad told me about you, I thought being aggressive would work. Did I scare you?" She took a swig of her beer and looked up at him. "*Am* I scaring you?"

What scared him was how she turned him on with what appeared to be no effort at all.

She didn't avert her gaze. "Or is it something else?"

Her openness spoke to him on a level he didn't realize he had—he'd tried hard to remain vacant beneath the surface.

"I know I'm not your type, but maybe you're not attracted to me at all. I mean, I know I'm a lot of woman for some men." Her effort at a joke didn't mask her insecurity, as she meant for it to do.

This was his opening. He'd tell her he couldn't do it, and it would all be over. He shouldn't feel bad about turning her down. He wasn't supposed to be attracted to her anyway.

"No." His voice sounded choked, so he had to repeat it. "No. You're not my type.

She nodded, but he didn't stop talking, though he knew what came out of his mouth next could ruin everything. "And it's not just your looks. You're loud and opinionated and nosy. You always have a snarky comeback at the ready, and you flaunt your sexuality like a flag. You're nothing like the women I go for, which only makes it worse."

"Okay, now you're being an ass. Saying you're not into me was enough. Let me show you outside. You can wait for Brad downstairs." She stood and pushed past him, but he grabbed her arm.

"But I never said I wasn't into you. I could have told Brad you just don't do it for me, but I didn't. Because it would be a lie."

Becca opened her mouth to respond. Closed it again. Chewed on her lower lip. "So…"

"So if you weren't his girlfriend, I'd fuck you right here. Now. I'd make you come again and again. Scream my name until you lost your voice. But you are his, Becca. If you were my type, I'd attribute it to casual attraction and go blow my load elsewhere, but there's nothing casual about this. We go through with this three-way, and at least one of us gets hurt, and I don't— I can't."

She smiled, and the line between her brows smoothed out. "Too many ifs. Too many worries. If we do it and like it, we can always keep doing it."

His heart leapt up his throat. "Brad never mentioned that was a possibility. He said you just wanted to try it."

She wrapped her fingers around his wrist, and loosened his grasp so she could slip free. "What's the use of trying something, if you can't have it again?" She turned and stepped on the mattress.

"What are you doing?" He knew the answer.

"You can try me now."

"But Brad—"

"Brad likes to watch. Sometimes he likes to record too." She giggled at his shocked expression. "You didn't know that? There's all sorts of things Brad likes that he hasn't shared with you. Yet."

"Like Becca," Brad said from behind him.

Colin hadn't even heard the apartment door open and close.

In front of him, Becca stretched and undulated her hips, dancing to the rhythm of a song he couldn't hear. Brad's heavy palms landed on Colin's shoulders, and Colin's pulse sped up. His breaths came short and shallow.

"Don't you want her?" Brad whispered in his ear. "If you don't, I'll take her and you can watch again. Or you can walk away."

Becca did that magical thing women did, and took off her bra without removing her shirt. She tossed it to Colin in a pink blur of satin and lace. "Which will it be?"

Colin wanted this, but he wasn't ready. He had to think. Becca said there could be more than one night, but what part would he be expected to play? Would they all be fucking casually? Would Brad and Becca call him when they felt like it?

More?

Becca removed a pin from her bun and shook her head. Her hair tumbled down her shoulders in the unruly mess Colin had come to find irresistible. She grasped the hem of her shirt with both hands and pinned Colin with her gaze. "Well? In or out?"

"I'm in." He'd so regret this.

Chapter Eight

Becca glanced behind Colin, and must have liked what she saw on Brad's face, because a lascivious smile blossomed slowly on her lips.

He was already hard, but her smile made his erection throb almost painfully.

She raised her shirt inch by inch, watching him watch her. The worn fabric slid upward, revealing pale skin marred around her stomach by a few pink stretch marks.

Becca sucked in her stomach, and Colin felt like an idiot for even noticing the marks, when he could be feeling the soft flesh instead.

Conscious of Brad watching, Colin tried not to appear too eager as he approached her. He stopped just short of the mattress, and spread his palms on her sides, caressing her belly with his thumbs. She still stood a few inches shorter than him and looked up with a tiny shiver.

"Don't." He pulled her shirt the rest of the way up and helped her slip it off, mesmerized by the sway of her breasts. Her areolas were lighter than he expected, but her nipples looked biteable. His mouth watered, and he swallowed before managing to speak again. "I want *you*. If I were looking for something different, I wouldn't be here."

Looking back, he couldn't tell when the playful atmosphere turned sticky with desire and hidden passions, but she wasn't smiling when she nodded. She squared her shoulders and raised her chin defiantly.

She put herself on display for him, and Colin didn't shy away. He took it all in. The roundness of her shoulders and arms, her ample breasts, her wide waist and jutting stomach. Until that moment, he expected to like and want her despite her body, but the fullness of her breasts made his mouth water. She was supple and yielding, soft and warm, and he liked her body as it was—not flawed, but inviting.

He traced her stretch marks with his fingertips, and she batted his hand away.

Behind him, Brad said, "Let him know all of you, Becca. See what he's been missing."

His voice broke the spell, and Becca smiled again. "It's a lot to see. Are you sure he's ready?"

Colin wouldn't be talked about like he wasn't there. He enjoyed Becca's surprised gasp when he clasped her shorts and undid their fly, before shoving them down her legs.

He took a step back and kept studying her. Her legs were toned, as he already knew, but what pulled his gaze was the naked triangle at the apex of her fleshy thighs. She was smooth, and he had to taste her. But first, she had to know what she did to him.

"You're beautiful," he said, trying to let his honesty show in his eyes.

"And what are you going to do about it?" Her usual good cheer had filled in for her moment of insecurity, but didn't erase it from Colin's mind.

In that moment, he thought he'd die before he made her feel unsure of herself again.

"Worship you." He sank to his knees in front of her and relished her little squeal of delight. Grabbing a handful of ass cheek in each palm, he buried his face between her legs and inhaled deeply.

"That tickles." But she held his head to her and tilted her pelvis, so his nose rubbed against her mons.

Colin traced her slit with the tip of his tongue, barely applying any pressure. Becca stood perfectly still, but he felt her tension. He ran his tongue along her opening once more, just as lightly, and this time she thrust her hips forward.

"I expected worshiping to be more fervent," she said through gritted teeth.

Colin meant to draw out his teasing, but Brad said, "Maybe you should lie down, so he can see the temple better." He sounded pained.

Colin looked over his shoulder and saw Brad had pulled his cock out and was stroking it.

Becca glanced from one to the other and knelt too, mirroring Colin. "There's something I want to do first."

Before Colin could ask what that was, she cupped the back of his head and slanted her lips over his. Just like the rest of her, her lips were pliable and warm, and Colin wondered how they would feel wrapped around his cock. As if she read his mind, she sucked his tongue into her mouth. He groaned and let his hands roam down her back and up her sides, until each of his palms cradled a heavy breast.

He broke the kiss and studied her face as he kneaded each mound gently. Her eyes were closed, her lips forming a silent 'O'.

Her pussy would have to wait.

He ducked his head and kissed the hollow of her neck, nibbling on the skin before licking a trail down to one nipple. He nuzzled it with his nose, feeling it harden against him, and then rolled it with his open palm.

Becca moaned, and Brad's panting reached Colin's ears. He didn't like that Brad was so far away, but after Colin had resisted a threesome for so long, he couldn't invite Brad to join him and Becca. Not just yet.

He returned his focus to Becca's breasts and closed his teeth gently over the second nipple. Becca inhaled sharply, and he bit again, a little harder. He loved how responsive she was. Loved making her respond to him. After being the prey in their cat and mouse game this long, he finally felt like he called the shots.

Becca had a different idea. She placed both hands on top of his head and pushed him downward, while at the same time scooting back. Following her body, Colin crawled on the mattress with her, and he made himself comfortable between her spread thighs, mindless of wrinkling his button-down shirt and his slacks.

"That's it," Brad said. "Eat her out."

Colin obeyed, ignoring the part of his brain that said he was just their toy. He used his thumbs to open her up to his hungry gaze, and savored the sight of the glistening pink flesh. The first long swipe of his tongue had Becca's hips flying off the mattress, but he pressed his elbows on her legs to pin her in place, and kept licking and sucking until she said she couldn't take any more.

And then he went on a little longer.

She scratched at his head, her fingers seeking purchase, but not managing to grasp the short cropped hair. Her thighs stressed and trembled with the effort to close, to move her away from his mouth, but he latched his lips on her clitoris and pushed two fingers inside her pussy. It made her buck even harder.

"Do you want me to stop?" His words came back to him muffled.

"Uh-uh," Becca managed.

He heard footsteps approaching and glanced to the side, to see Brad kneeling by Becca's head. He was stark naked. A light sheen of sweat covered his sculpted chest and abs, and matted the thatch of dark curls at the base of his cock. His neck was corded with the strain of holding back his release, as he worked his fist leisurely up and down his shaft.

Colin kept finger fucking Brad's girlfriend, while he studied Brad's cock—it was shorter than Colin's, but thicker, the head darker.

Colin gulped. Was Brad about to join them? Where was he planning on sticking his dick?

Panic warred with hope and desire. Colin didn't know if he wanted Brad to shove his cock down Becca's throat or in Colin's own ass, or if he preferred to have Becca to himself this once.

His cock was apparently happy with any possible outcome. He thrust his hips against the mattress, to achieve some friction. It only made things worse. He needed to come, or he'd burst.

"I'm not going to touch her," Brad said. "I just want to see her come. She's gorgeous when she comes, Colin."

Colin didn't reply, but added another finger inside Becca, stretching her. She contracted around him, but didn't move other than that, apparently exhausted. It was time to finish her off. He curved his fingers upward and flexed them in a come-hither motion, at the same time he grazed his teeth against her clit.

Becca's back arched, her entire body clenching and relaxing in rapid succession. Her head fell back, and she let out a keening sound that probably carried to the ground floor.

Colin couldn't wait to pull that sound out of her again.

He jumped up and fumbled with his belt buckle until he finally unclasped it, popped his button, and slid down the zipper of his slacks. He was aware he was rushing more than he had since his very first fuck, but he needed to be inside Becca *now*. He had to take a deep breath and force himself to slow down. He undid the first two buttons of his shirt and then his cuffs, and pulled it over his head.

Any self-control he'd managed to regain evaporated when he saw the naked hunger in Becca's eyes. Her gaze slid down his torso like a caress that set his skin on fire. What had him kicking off his loafers and shoving the pants down his thighs was the matching look on Brad's face. Brad licked his lips, and Colin wanted to feel those lips on his cock as much as he wanted to sink inside Becca's pussy.

He barely had enough presence of mind to lose the socks before his slacks came off completely. Like Becca, he went commando, so there was no underwear to remove, but…

"Condom. Fuck." He reached for the pocket of the trousers bunched on the floor behind him.

"I'm on the pill," Becca said. "Haven't been with anyone but Brad since we got together, and I'm clean." She laughed. "Now, can you please take a breath? There's no rush."

Colin *never* had unprotected sex. He never believed girls who said they were on the pill, and didn't think there was a situation pressing enough that he'd risk catching something from a potential partner. But it was different with Becca.

Without a word, he lay by her side, hauled her closer, and gave her a deep, lingering kiss. "No rush for you. I need to fuck you as soon as possible."

Her grin reappeared, wider than before. "How do you want me?"

"I want you to ride me." Holding her to him, he rolled on his back, so her body covered his. The position brought him close to Brad's dripping cock, and also allowed him to see all of Becca, as she lifted her lips, positioned him at her entrance, and lowered herself on his cock.

Fuck it felt good being inside her. He watched her backside in the mirror, her full buttocks rippling every time she slapped down on him. He watched his own fingers dig inside the firm flesh of her ass, while he felt her nails gouge his arms. Becca met every thrust of his hips and matched him moan for moan. She dipped her head down for a kiss and bit his lower lip until he thought he'd bleed, and still her hips danced to his music and drove him crazy with the need for release.

Next to him, Brad's head was tilted back, his mouth open, his hand a blur of movement on his cock. Colin was never much into sucking cock, but he wouldn't mind tasting Brad's.

He let the fantasy of being sandwiched between Becca and Brad pull him in and then under, and lost himself in the possibilities now open before him. Above him, Becca kept undulating and drawing his orgasm ever closer, and next to him his best friend was bringing himself off at the visual of Colin fucking his girlfriend.

His body and mind were on overdrive, and the abundance of stimuli threatened to send him over the edge before he had the time to bring Becca off. With the last dregs of his self-control, he snaked his hand to where her body met his, and pressed his thumb on her clit, pistoning his hips faster.

Her whole body shuddered, her nails raising welts on his chest as she clenched around his cock until he could no longer hold back. Grinding his pelvis to hers, he matched her unraveling. His legs shook, his arms felt made of lead, and he could barely keep his eyes open, but his cock still sent spurts of cum inside her. She fell forward and kissed him again, her hair tickling his chin.

"Baby," Brad whispered, and Becca disentangled herself from Colin to suck her boyfriend off.

Colin let his eyes drift shut. Whatever happened from here on didn't involve him.

Chapter Nine

Colin's phone buzzed again. He glanced at it, opened the first drawer of his desk, and tossed it in. Didn't help much. Now his entire desk buzzed.

And if he kept not answering, Brad would show up at work or at his home or in his dreams, and mess him up more.

Colin had been screening Brad's calls for forty eight hours. Two days since he'd had a taste of Becca, and she still lingered on his lips, on his body, and on his mind.

Correction—*they* still lingered, hovered around him, driving him up the walls with the need for more.

But he couldn't have more.

Once he and Becca were done fucking, she'd gone to Brad, because she was his, and he was hers, and Colin was the odd man out. He'd gathered his clothes and slinked to the other room to get dressed. Brad called for him, but Colin knew his part was done. There was no reason to prolong his goodbye.

He let out a bitter chuckle. This should be his dream situation. Amazing fucking with no cuddling afterward. No strings attached. No expectations of him.

But there were strings—many of them—just thin and light, and he hadn't noticed them until they'd wrapped around him and pulled him in all directions.

What he'd done was wrong. Yes, Brad asked him to, and Becca practically begged for it, but this was the one time in his life he had to be the mature adult, and he'd screwed up. Brad was probably calling to tell him he was wrong, and he couldn't handle the memory of Colin and Becca together. That their friendship was over.

Maybe Brad had noticed how Colin responded to his naked body, and wanted to call him a fucking fag, like—

"Fuck." Colin hadn't realized the buzzing stopped, but he sure as hell noticed it start again. It vibrated up his arm, where he leaned on the desk. Didn't help his headache and made his teeth chatter.

It was short this time. A text.

Against his better judgment, he brought out the phone and read what Brad had sent.

> *Saturday @ 8, we'll be there.*
> *Waiting for you. It's her birthday,*
> *man. If you don't show, we'll*
> *pretend none of it ever happened.*
> *We go back to the way things were.*
> *I don't want to lose you. But we*
> *could have so much more.*

Colin hated the hope flitting in his chest. Words. It was just words. Brad never took no for an answer and would do anything to get his way. Including promising Colin something he'd never give him.

More.

Brad was straight laced. This was all Becca's idea, and Brad would go along until it bit him in the ass. Colin would gladly jump at the opportunity for a repeat now he knew how good a lay she was. But she was more than a good lay. She made him reconsider things he thought were set in stone. When she was around — when he even thought of her — he reverted into a horny teenager, instead of the experienced man he was.

She made him regret not having met her sooner.

And she brought forth a new, ferociously sexy side of timid Brad, that made Colin want to forget he ever chose friendship over sex.

If a single tryst led to them taking up his every waking thought, what would happen if he showed up Saturday? What would happen if he had more of Becca, if he felt Brad's cock rub against his own inside her, if he slipped and kissed Brad with all the passion Colin had felt on that mattress, surrounded by the two of them?

What would happen if he got hooked on them, only for Brad to decide he no longer wanted to share?

When Colin left them enveloped in each other's arms, he told himself he could keep it casual. The dull ache inside was just his body crashing from the high of fucking Becca. Sex this earth shattering was worth any cost, including future heartache. He'd repeat it as often they wanted and in any combination they decided.

By the time he'd reached home, the sex-induced haze had cleared, and his stomach churned. He'd crossed the line. He'd broken his own rule. He'd fucked his best friend's girlfriend, *in front of him*. And he'd do it again. He'd sacrifice his friendship with Brad, to feel Becca's pussy fluttering around him once more. He'd probably sacrifice a limb too, to be allowed to fuck Brad's virginal ass.

His head hurt, and his cock ached at the memory of his time with the couple.

He opened Brad's latest text and reread it.

If you don't show, we'll pretend none of it ever happened.

That was what Colin should do. Meeting them on Saturday would be nothing but trouble, and he didn't need more of that.

But he'd get to touch Becca one last time. His sweat would mix with Brad's on the sheets and on her skin. He'd hear their panted breaths, her mewls, his groans... the slapping of flesh on flesh.

The scent of sex that had suffused the room with the large windows and mirror ceiling filled his nostrils. *Their* scent.

Colin swallowed past the knot in his throat and adjusted his cock.

He really shouldn't go to them on Saturday.

No. He wouldn't.

Probably.

Brad

Chapter Ten

"He wasn't better than me?" Brad trailed his fingers along Becca's thigh. He'd managed not to ask for almost the entire Saturday, but he had to know.

She propped herself up and looked down at him with a sly smile. "Best post-coital line ever. Were you thinking of Colin the whole time?"

Brad enjoyed the weight of her breasts pressing into his chest. He tangled his fingers in her wild hair and pulled her to him for a deep kiss he hoped conveyed how mind blowing sex with her was. "I can't think of anything when I'm inside you. You know that." He bucked his hips, to stress his point.

"Good." She nuzzled his neck.

A few seconds ticked by, before he asked, "So, was he?"

Becca cracked up. "I knew you wouldn't let it go." She rolled to the side, but kept touching him, drawing circles on his skin, playing with the line of hair beneath his navel.

If he weren't completely drained, he'd go for another round. "That's not an answer."

"Do you want an answer?"

He turned to face her. "I do. I want to know what he did better, so I can top him next time." Becca arched an eyebrow, and he grinned. She always made him smile or grin or laugh. He couldn't get enough of her.

"Okay, if it's to get me even better sex. He was different. Seemed more sure of himself, and at the same time his touch was less confident. It was… different."

"I can be different." He cupped one of her breasts and grazed the nipple with the pad of his thumb.

"You don't have to. You're you, and Colin's not. I like sex with both of you, which I thought was the point of what we asked him to do. Am I wrong?" Her tone had lost the playfulness it conveyed till now, and she studied him intensely. A vertical line creased her forehead. Was she worried or upset?

Brad caught her gaze and held it, while he sought the answer to her question. Yes, the point was for her to have sex she'd love with two different men. It was her fantasy he wanted to fulfill. Because it was all supposed to be about her. Not about Brad's need to get closer to Colin, by sharing the woman he loved with him.

And how long would Brad be able to sit on that last bit of information? The words had jumped to his lips all the more often since he watched her with Colin, but he wanted saying them to be special.

"You're not wrong." He tucked a strand of Becca's curly hair behind her ear. He loved her hair. Loved how she used it to caress his stomach when she went down on him. Loved tugging on it, as he took her against the window, for the world to see that she was his and his alone.

How could he be so possessive of her, yet ache to share her as much as she wanted to be shared — if not more? "I want to give you your wish for your birthday," he said and felt like a dirty liar.

Her expression remained serious. "I don't want you to do this for me, if you're not a thousand percent on board. Yes, Colin is gorgeous… " Brad narrowed his eyes, and she glared. "You know he's stunning. You can see it. The man is an Adonis. That face belongs on the cover of a magazine, and his body — "

"Enough with singing his praise. Make your point, please."

"My point is he's not my boyfriend. You are. He is really good in bed, or on the floor, but if you're not okay with it, he doesn't have to join us. Not on my birthday, not ever."

Brad nodded, trying to ignore the disappointment in her tone. She liked Colin more than she let on. Wanted to be with him again. But she wouldn't, if Brad didn't want her to.

He already offered Colin an out — gave him the option to pretend his time with Becca never happened. This was Brad's out, his chance to draw a line between his relationship with Becca and his friendship with Colin, and keep them separate for good. To protect all three of them from the harm Colin warned him about. To keep things as safe as possible.

If he wanted to.

But he didn't.

Colin fucking Becca had been the most erotic thing Brad had ever seen. He knew how she gave herself to her lover, but he'd never watched Colin open up like this before. The way Colin approached Becca, the way he took her in before he actually took her, had betrayed a vulnerability completely unlike him. It had turned Brad on more than he'd considered possible.

As if that wasn't weird enough, there was the little matter of jealousy. Brad had expected to be jealous that another man touched Becca, but not also because Becca was lucky enough to feel Colin naked against her. Heck, why would he consider that 'lucky'? It was so confusing, seeing them writhe together and not knowing whose place he'd rather be in.

"You don't have to decide right now."

Had she read his mind? No, wait. They were talking about something.

"Just know that whether we go through with it or not is completely up to you."

"Okay." He feathered his fingers over her hipbone, but she batted his hand away.

"No more nookie for tonight. You promised to take me dancing."

He had, darn it. He'd much rather stay in bed with her than get up and get dressed, only to join the sea of people that thought there was something inherently wrong with spending a Saturday night at home. "Right," he said hoping she'd catch on to his lack of enthusiasm and let him off the hook.

Becca clucked her tongue. "I don't do sulky boys."

"Who's sulky? I can't wait for a night of clubbing." Brad jumped out of bed and rushed to the shower, Becca's crystalline laugh trailing after him.

* * * *

Brad took another swig of his beer and pretended to laugh at something the big lug next to him said. Brad couldn't imagine what Becca's best friend saw in the guy, but the two had been engaged for a while and seemed happy. Mostly. Big Lug didn't look all that happy to be there.

Brad couldn't blame him. He wasn't into clubs either, but he'd do anything for Becca. Including share her with his best friend.

And he wasn't going to think of Colin again tonight.

He'd stay in the moment.

This wasn't so bad.

Sure, the place was packed and smelled of sweat, but Becca was on the dance floor, doing her best to make him forget about his surroundings—and succeeding. She threw her arms around Amanda's neck and swished her ass to the rhythm of the music. Brad knew it was for his benefit. He smiled and shook his head. "That girl is driving me crazy."

Big Lug, also known as Mason, nodded. "I don't know how you put up with these displays, man. If she were my woman—"

"Well, she's not." Brad cut him a glance that shut him up. Yeah, this engagement was a mystery to him. The petite blonde dancing with Becca was a hellion, and her fiancé was dull as a doorknob, as well as apparently stuck in the nineteen-fifties.

"I'm going to get another drink." Mason hightailed it to the bar, and Brad sighed. The air seemed lighter without Mason's brooding.

"He's a breath of fresh air, huh?" A tall brunette clunked her glass against Brad's bottle and gave him a beaming smile.

"Yeah… " What was the etiquette here? Was she just making polite chit chat or flirting? Clubs were mating grounds, in his limited experience. Should he straight up tell her he was seeing someone? "I'm—"

"Brad. I know." Her smile widened, and he noticed her eyes. They looked just like Amanda's.

"You're Amanda's little sister," he said as much to her as to himself.

"*And* I've got a name. Alice." She tipped an imaginary hat.

Relaxed, he returned her smile and held out his free hand. "Nice to meet you, Alice."

She closed her palm around his and pulled him close. "You too." Her cheerful tone never changed, as she added, "You break her heart, and I'll end you."

His first instinct was to assure her he wouldn't, but he wasn't opening his heart to a stranger. "Good to know." And Becca had seriously cool friends.

"So how come you're not there, dancing with our girl?" Alice asked.

"I don't dance." He glanced at Becca. She faced his way now, eyes closed, wisps of curly hair plastered to her cheeks. She undulated more than swayed, her every move tugging at his groin. "Actually, do you mind?" he asked.

"Go ahead." Alice tilted her head toward the dancing crowd.

Brad strode toward Becca, taking in every detail. God, she was beautiful. Her eyes were what had first stolen his heart. She called them hazel, but there were flecks of gold in them that made them shine. Bright eyes. And her smile… those plump lips arching in a teasing curve under a perfect Cupid's bow sent jolts of desire straight to his cock. As did the way she bunched the hem of her burgundy mini dress in her fists and lifted it above mid-thigh. Two inches higher, and he'd see her bare pussy. His mouth watered at the thought.

Amanda smirked and nodded to him. She said something to Becca, who didn't stop moving, and left toward the bar.

Becca opened her eyes when Brad was a couple of feet away. She sucked her lower lip between her teeth. Her gaze was filled with a hunger matching Brad's.

He wrapped one arm around her waist and yanked her to him. Her large breasts flattened against his chest, and he was hard pressed not to wedge his free hand between their bodies, to feel her heat in his palm.

One corner of her lips twitched, and she stood on tiptoe. "Took you long enough," she whispered in his ear, her lips brushing the lobe.

Thirty-six long years, to be exact. "I'm here now."

"And what are you going to do?"

Brad moved his hips, so she could feel his erection digging into her belly. "Oh, I have an idea or two." He wanted to walk her backward to the nearest wall, lift her legs around his waist, and fuck her to the rhythm of the music blasting from the speakers. She'd probably be up for it, but her friends were nearby, and he wasn't yet at that level of not giving a fuck what people thought.

Still, he was working on building up his courage.

He devoured her mouth as he wanted to devour her cunt, sucking her tongue and biting her lips. Not breaking the kiss, he drove her further into the dancing crowd, getting bolder as more bodies were added to the pulsating wall hiding them from Amanda, Mason, and Alice. He cupped Becca's ass and kneaded the full flesh, sliding her dress higher in the process. The tips of his fingers touched naked skin, and he growled against her mouth. He wanted to feel more of her.

Becca tangled her fingers in his hair and pulled, her other hand a clamp around his bicep.

Screw it—he *was going* to feel more of her. With his thumb, he caressed her under the hem of the dress. Becca shivered. Her nipples grazed his chest. He wanted to pop one in his mouth, but that might be too much. Not that baring her ass in the middle of the dance floor wasn't, but he hoped nobody noticed that. Except maybe the guy behind her, who winked at him.

Brad nuzzled Becca's cheek. "We have an audience."

"Then let's give them a show."

Fuck, he loved this woman. He inched his palm between her legs and brushed his thumb along her slit. She was so wet, he considered going with his first plan anyway, but he doubted they'd make it to the wall, all the way across the room now. He squeezed her ass and snaked his hand lower again, this time to dip two fingers between her folds.

"More." Her breath was hot against his chin.

The angle was all wrong. He couldn't go as deep as he wanted to, unless he turned her with his back to him. But then her pussy would be exposed to everyone, and that was too much for him. One hand still on her ass, he slid the other one down her belly and pushed two fingers inside her.

Becca bucked her hips. "More."

The man behind her moved closer, but backed off when Brad scowled. Brad would share her with Colin, not with a random stranger.

"More," she said again, and he had to obey.

He started pumping his fingers inside her, drawing out her pleasure, but not touching her clit. She liked being teased, and he liked giving her what she wanted.

She rocked against his palm, but Brad denied her the friction she was after. He used his other hand to caress her ass from side to side, occasionally slipping his middle finger between her butt cheeks.

"You're naughty," she said.

"You love it." He slid his finger lower until he found her wetness and then trailed it upward, to circle her asshole. He hadn't been there before. Well, his fingers had, but she hadn't asked him to fuck her ass, and he didn't want to pressure her into anything.

Maybe this Saturday. Or maybe she'd want to be looking at him and have Colin behind her.

If Colin showed up.

Fucking Colin.

He massaged Becca's asshole with the tip of his finger, but didn't push in the tight ring of muscle.

She moaned and bit his earlobe. "In or out? The suspense is killing me."

He kept fucking her with his other hand, his elbow making impact with bodies brushing past them. His pulse pounded in his ears, drowning out the thudding of the music. Her perfume filled his nostrils, and he loved how she leaned her weight on him, as if her legs no longer held her.

"Which do you want?" he asked. "Do you want my finger in your ass? Do you want to come, while I fill both your holes with my hands?" Before Becca, he wouldn't dream of talking like this to a woman. Not without being stricken down by lightning. But his girl loved dirty talk.

Becca spread her thighs more. "I want you to be fucking me right here, surrounded by all these people. I want your cock inside me."

Maybe he loved dirty talk too. He'd tried hard to make this all about her, but his cock throbbed. When she glided her hand down his body to squeeze him through his pants, he thought he'd pop in her palm. "Come," he said. "I'll have my turn when we get home."

She looked at him and shook her head, but her eyes were glazed over.

Brad forced a third finger inside her cunt and pressed his thumb on her clit. "Now, Becca."

Her body tightened at the order, surprising him. He wasn't usually dominant with her. That part of him had only come out in the court room, back when he practiced law, and occasionally with an unruly crew member, but he was always putty in her hands.

He thought she wanted him easy going, but now he reconsidered.

And since he was rethinking things, he inched a finger inside her asshole too.

She convulsed so hard, for a moment he thought she meant to push him away. Her hips bucked, her legs trembling. She dropped her head into the crook of his shoulder and bit over his shirt, clenching his hands hard between her thighs and pulling on his hair.

When her orgasm finally subsided, he helped her steady herself and straighten her dress. His cock was about to rip through his zipper, and he had to hold it through the pocket of his slacks, so it didn't nudge people as he and Becca made their way back to her friends.

Becca's flushed face could be due to vigorous dancing, but Amanda and Alice shared a smirk. Mason looked constipated, so nothing out of the ordinary. Minutes later, he and Amanda said goodnight. Alice declared she was going fishing, and got lost among the throng of dancing bodies.

"You ready to go?" Becca asked.

Brad didn't bother answering. He grabbed her hand and made a beeline to the exit.

They had sex in the back seat of his car, like teenagers, laughing the entire time.

Chapter Eleven

Brad hadn't checked his phone all evening. It hadn't been a conscious decision; he'd just been too busy being into Becca, as well as inside her, to wonder if Colin had called or texted.

"Nothing. Asshole is stuck on this radio-silence thing." He all but threw the cell phone on his nightstand and toed off his loafers.

Becca was already in bed. "He'll call. Come to bed." She patted the empty side of the mattress. She hadn't bothered removing her makeup and looked adorably disheveled.

Brad sat on the bed and leaned in for a quick kiss. He slipped off his socks and undid his pants. He didn't bother unbuttoning his shirt — just the collar, before pulling it over his head and throwing it across the room. It landed on the armchair in the corner and was soon followed by his slacks.

He slid under the covers, enjoying the cool fabric against his naked skin. No-clothes-in-bed was Becca's idea, and he'd taken to it like a fish to water.

She draped one thigh over his, and he ghosted his fingertips up her leg. "Your skin is like silk."

She mmm-ed.

How could Colin touch her and not want seconds? How could he have been inside her and not jump at the opportunity to do it again? Brad's cock stirred. He circled her wrist with his fingers and led her hand to his cock. "I love touching you."

Becca's eyes drifted shut. "I need to sleep. You never let me sleep, you insatiable man."

"I can't help myself around you." He kissed the tip of her nose "Goodnight, babe." *I love you* was at the tip of his tongue, but he bit it back for now. If Colin wasn't going to show on Saturday, Brad would still need to make her day special, so he'd keep his declaration of love to himself till then.

She turned her back to him and scooched closer, fitting perfectly into the curve of his body. "Sleep. No more thinking. Gives you wrinkles, and I like my boys smooth."

Smooth. Like Colin's chest. Colin insisted he didn't wax, but he did something. No way was Golden Boy's torso naturally hairless. Knowing Colin's obsession with beauty, Brad wouldn't put it past him to spend hours making sure he looked flawless.

Which he did. Brad had seen Colin naked before Friday—they visited the same gym, and Colin wasn't one for modesty—but he hadn't exactly been able to study him. It wouldn't have been kosher to be caught ogling his best friend in the lockers or the showers. Besides, Brad never before had the urge to look, either.

Liar.

Okay, maybe once or twice. When Colin opened up about his sexuality, Brad wasn't shocked, but he couldn't understand how someone who was interested in smooth creatures with boobs and a pussy could also be interested in hard muscle, wide shoulders, coarse-haired thighs, and... cock. He tried to see what his best friend saw in the male form.

It was possible he tried too hard, because he'd started recognizing the beauty of the sculpted planes of Colin's body, if not appreciate them the way he did Becca's soft curves. Brad told himself he was so secure in his sexuality, he could admit that he found a guy attractive.

So that guy was his best friend — so what?

It didn't mean Brad wanted to fuck Colin.

It just meant Brad had to hide the mother of all erections when Colin tried to scare him off the threesome by warning him their cocks would rub against each other, their balls slapping together.

He wiped the sleep from his eyes and gently disentangled himself from Becca.

"Where are you going?" she mumbled, half asleep.

"To get some water. Be right back." Yup. He'd get a glass of water. And maybe call Colin once more.

Becca reached for him blindly. "Let the man get some rest, baby. It's late."

She knew him so well and accepted all of him. Maybe she'd accept his secret fantasies too, if he found the courage to put them into words. Or to even consciously think of them.

For now, they were fragmented mental images of helping Colin wash his back in the shower. Touching

Colin's thigh. Pumping Colin's cock and leading it to Becca's pussy.

Merely admiring the human form wasn't a sin, was it? It had been too long since he read the bible, but he'd remember that. Then again, pure admiration didn't come with lustful thoughts like the ones he entertained, and he was pretty fucking sure those were sinful. As was pretty much everything he did with Becca, so maybe he should stop worrying God cared what Brad did in and out of bed with a willing partner.

Of either sex.

Yeah, well, even if God didn't care, Brad's mother would.

He didn't use a glass. Just opened the faucet and cupped his hand under the running water. He gulped eagerly, to satiate his thirst, and then splashed some on his face. It did nothing for his burning skin.

His mother didn't have to know. Not like they talked about whom Brad had sex with. She was as good at pretending Brad was innocent as he was at pretending the check she gave the church once a year made her a good person.

And this was a dark path to go down, so he dredged his thoughts back to the question that burned him.

Was he gay? Was that why he had the thoughts he did for Colin? No straight man wondered how another man's mouth tasted.

Then why was he so drawn to Becca? Why did he want to have her as often as possible? It wasn't overcompensating; a whiff of her perfume was enough to get him hard. He wanted her and was determined to tell her he loved her. He'd cook her dinner this Saturday, open his heart to her, and then give her her gift—assuming Colin showed up.

The way she took over for Colin in Brad's head was a relief. He wasn't gay. Wasn't fooling himself and his partner. The most possible scenario was that his sexuality, repressed by his strict upbringing, had finally found an outlet in this amazing, wild woman, and he wanted to soak up new experiences. Which made him bi-curious. It sounded better, not that he'd say it aloud. His mother would disown him. And possibly sue the Catholic all-boys school Brad had attended.

More confusion. He'd never entertained impure thoughts about any of his classmates, and not for lack of opportunity. The communal showers should have clued him in, if he were the tiniest bit into guys.

So why did he keep calling Colin?

He returned to bed, hoping to will away his returning erection.

Sleep would do him some good, but Becca's warm naked body beside him sent his thoughts back to that apartment with the mattress on the floor and the mirrors on the ceiling.

Becca's body wrapped around Colin's, her pale flesh glowing against his golden skin. His hardness melting into her soft curves. Together they were perfection, and Brad wanted to have them both, at least once.

Shit.

Chapter Twelve

"Stop checking your phone, and go. You're already an hour late."

Brad looked at Becca stretching on the bed. Her naked shoulder and thigh peeked out from under the covers, and her hair was strewn around her head in a dark, messy halo. Knowing what the sheets kept from him wasn't conducive to getting his ass to the office, even if he'd spent the greatest part of Sunday in bed with her.

He should have spent *all* of Sunday in bed with her. Then he wouldn't have sent Colin that stupid text.

"You're looking at me like I'm breakfast." Becca rolled on her side and tucked more of the covers between her legs, revealing a round buttock. How did he ever think he was gay, when he wanted to do unspeakable, wicked things to her ass?

Maybe he could spare another half hour? "I can see you covered in maple syrup. Or whipped cream." He waggled his eyebrows.

"Messy, but sounds good. I may be convinced, if you throw in a bubble bath afterward."

"Deal." He slid on a dark blue tie and turned to the full-size mirror to do the knot. This was who he'd been before Becca waltzed into his life in her silly stained overalls and perfect manicure. He'd been Mr. Poised, and she'd been Ms. Crazy-Pants. Who'd have thought he'd end up head over heels for her — or with her heels by his head within hours of first meeting her outside his company?

She'd told him she was new in town and asked if he knew a good cocktail bar. In a surprisingly bold move, he'd invited her to dinner at an Italian restaurant he knew. That first date had been a series of surprises.

Becca had turned out to be his newest employee. And born and raised right there, in San Francisco. She'd lied, because he was hot, as she admitted. He'd been unable to take his eyes off her lips while she spoke.

"My place or yours?" she'd asked him before they were done with their starters.

He'd spluttered and gone against every principle he'd been brought up with. "Mine." It was the first time he'd had sex outside a loving, committed relationship.

He wouldn't trade it for this world or the next one.

"My place or yours?" he asked now with a smile.

"Mine," Becca said. "Have to spend some time with Ms. Thing, before she goes cat-ninja on my furniture. Say nine?"

"I'll bring dinner."

"I'll provide the entertainment." She inched to the edge of the bed, and he leaned down for a quick kiss. She'd go back to sleep as soon as he was gone. "And give Colin some time. He needs to process things," she said.

"He's a guy, Becca. We don't take as long to process as you do." Blatant lie, because Brad was still processing and probably would be for a while. He considered sending Colin another quick text, but what could he say this time?

He shoved his phone in his back pocket and grabbed his jacket and briefcase. He was dragging his feet. Though he generally felt reluctant to leave Becca in the morning, it had been a while since he felt this miserable. She'd brought a bounce to his step, and a night with her felt like drinking from the fountain of youth. He only wished Colin felt the same way.

About Brad's girlfriend.

And Brad accused *Colin* of being a sick fuck.

Maybe he should go spill his guts to Father Aloysius and leave the whole mess behind. But that would mean no more fun sexy times with Becca either, and he wasn't willing to lose that.

"Give him time. And stop calling him." Becca's drowsy voice followed him to the front door.

"I'll try." He got out and locked the door behind him. Becca had her own set of keys. He gave it to her their first week together, completely astonishing both her and himself. But that was Becca. She was astonishing, and he was a new man because of her. One unafraid of his flaws and passions.

Less afraid, in any case.

He called the elevator and pulled out his phone for a quick glance at the time. Not to check if Colin had called or texted and he'd somehow missed it.

Nothing from Colin.

And it was a little after nine.

Shit.

As general manager of the construction company, Brad could make his own schedule, but he liked going in early, to set an example for employees. He didn't have to work on actual construction, but 'early' still meant eight in the morning. Today he wouldn't make it there before ten.

And that didn't account for the traffic he encountered as soon as he pulled out of the underground parking. Not an unusual phenomenon in San Francisco, but today in particular, he didn't want to be stuck in his car with his phone.

Eh. Resistance was futile. He fished his cell out of his pocket and pressed the side button to light the screen. Still nothing. Colin was such an ass some times. If he regretted what happened or just meant to write it off, he could at least text back to tell Brad to go screw himself. Or to leave him alone. Or something. Brad thought their friendship merited at least that courtesy. Anything but this damned disappearing act.

But no. Mr. Colin Daniels was treating Brad and Becca as he would a casual hookup. He wrote off all that came before he did, and deleted the girl's number.

In this case, Brad's number, since he didn't have Becca's.

Brad didn't tell Becca he suspected Colin was blowing them off. He'd rather let her think Colin was freaked out by the magnitude of what they'd done than tell her his best friend had taken what he wanted and had no more use for them.

His best friend. The man had been *his best friend* for six years. They'd shared so much, and now that Brad shared Becca with him, Colin acted like the love 'em-and-leave 'em type he always was. It shouldn't surprise Brad, but it did.

More, it pissed him off.

At the next traffic light, he browsed through his Sent folder and reread what he wrote the night before.

Saturday @ 8, we'll be there.
Waiting for you. It's her birthday,
man. If you don't show, we'll
pretend none of it ever happened.
We go back to the way things were.
I don't want to lose you. But we
could have so much more.

The last line had been an afterthought, a spur-of-the-moment thing. Brad hadn't mentioned it to Becca, because he wasn't sure what it meant. What was the 'more' he offered Colin? When he'd typed the words, they were meant to entice. A verbal nudge and wink for all the good times the three of them could share. But it wasn't phrased that way. It read like the vague promise of something deeper, and that wasn't Brad's to offer.

He wasn't certain he could — *would* — offer it, even if the choice were in his hands.

He sent, "At least tell me we're okay, you fucker."

There. Non-sentimental guy talk. His phone buzzed almost instantly with an answer. The light turned green, but Brad opened the text, ignoring the honking behind him.

We're okay, you fucker.

Brad snorted and tossed the phone on the passenger seat. They'd be fine. They might never be naked in the same room again, but they'd be fine.

And maybe Becca was right, and Colin was still processing.

* * * *

As per usual, Sarah fell in step with him the moment he exited the elevator. Part of her formidable assistant powers was the uncanny ability to guess the exact moment he'd show up at work. Either that, or she spent her mornings watching the closed-circuit camera that covered the garage.

"You're late." She crossed her arms. "Your mother has called twice."

Brad groaned. "Did you tell her I wasn't in?"

"What do you take me for? First time, I said you were on site, and second that you had a meeting."

"With whom?"

"The painting crew." She bit her lower lip, but not before Brad saw her grin.

"Nice, Sarah. Might as well have told her I was getting laid."

"I'll keep that in mind for next time." This time, she beamed a smile his way. It made her look eighteen.

He arched an eyebrow. "Your hair is a mess." It wasn't. The strawberry-blond, shoulder-length tresses were pulled back in the same perfectly tight bun as always, but the comment got her scattering to the bathroom and gave him time to sit at his desk and switch on his computer.

"My hair looks perfect," Sarah said with a mock scowl when she returned.

"As does the rest of you." She was his type, plump and bubbly, but with a killer wit. She also had a girlfriend she adored, and she knew Brad didn't mean his mock flirting.

"Yeah, yeah. You can't touch this."

"So what did my mother want?" Indubitably, to bust his balls about something, but he couldn't think what. Correction—he had some idea, judging from the snide remarks she'd repeatedly made about Becca, but he didn't have a fuck to spare on his mother's issues with his girlfriend.

"She said she needs to talk to you in person. She'll be by at six."

And his day kept getting better. "You couldn't talk her out of it?"

"I didn't try. You're a big boy; you can handle an hour with your mother."

"One of these days, I'll fire your ass." Never. At thirty two, she was four years younger than him, but she'd been his mother's assistant before he took the reins of the company, and she knew the business better than he did.

"You won't fire me, 'cause I can anticipate your needs. And right now, you need coffee."

Brad watched, as she left his office and closed the heavy double doors behind her. Then he turned his attention to his email, and his mood plummeted. Why couldn't Mondays be a little slower?

With the exception of a short break to have his tuna on rye, Brad kept himself busy until a little after four, making arrangements for upcoming projects and resolving issues with current ones.

His phone stayed quiet, but Colin's flippant reply to Brad's pissed-off text had cooled him down. Things were all right between him and Colin. Colin didn't want to discuss the other night, and that was fine. Brad would stop bugging him about it and trying to convince him to give a repeat performance. He probably shouldn't have called so many times to begin with. He should have trusted Colin not to be a prick when it came to him.

And really, Brad was the prick, for setting up Colin in a situation that obviously made him uncomfortable, but nothing would make him regret watching Becca and Colin light the sheets on fire. Yes, he was aware that made him a horrible friend.

As his workday slowed down, doubt inched its way into Brad's thoughts. Colin said they were okay, but that would probably be his reply to any chick who kept texting him after they had sex. Brad needed to see him up close, to make sure Colin wasn't avoiding him, like he would any random one-night stand.

But *they* didn't have sex. Colin had sex with Becca. She seduced him with Brad's blessings, and Colin seemed extremely into it, despite his initial reluctance. Maybe Brad should have given him more time to get used to the idea, before throwing him in an empty apartment with Becca and her irresistible charm.

That could be the problem—Colin felt forced into it, and he was now dealing with what he perceived as being used.

Brad had to talk to him. And not over the phone.

He looked at the time. Five twenty six. He was supposed to be in the office all day. His mother wouldn't like being stood up, and he wanted to show her what they'd done with the development in Mosso, anyway. He'd been running the company since she'd passed it to him on his thirty-fifth birthday, but more than a year later, he still felt the need to prove himself to her every chance he got.

He'd have to pass on that chance today. A bummer, because the apartment building was his best work so far, but Colin would be at the gym at six, if he stuck to his usual schedule.

"Where are you going?" Sarah jumped in front of him as he neared her desk. "Mrs. Miller will be here in an hour."

"Not if you call her now and tell her I had to step out."

"You know she doesn't like it when you cancel."

"My mother doesn't like *anything*, Sarah. She just accepts things grudgingly, when she's not presented with another choice." He held up an index finger and slipped past her. "Don't reschedule. Say I'll call her."

"You owe me for this."

"Put it on my tab." He all but ran to the elevator, waving at her over his shoulder.

Chapter Thirteen

Brad felt completely out of place at the gym, in his tailored suit and patent-leather shoes. He should have thought to bring a backpack with. At least pretend he was there to work out.

He made his way through treadmills and stationary bikes, trying not to make eye-contact with anyone. His phone buzzed repeatedly. His mother was probably not happy with the last-minute change of plans. Not his top priority.

He pushed into the men's changing rooms and spotted Colin immediately. He was fresh out of the shower, his wet hair gleaming bronze rather than its usual gold. His back was to the entrance, which gave Brad a couple of seconds to compose himself — and, okay, maybe study the wide back and narrow waist. Becca was right. Objectively speaking, Colin was gorgeous.

Brad crossed the room and stopped right behind him. "I knew you'd be here."

"Fuck." Colin jumped around, tightening the towel around his waist. His foot slipped, and he clutched at Brad's shoulder to find his balance. "Are you stalking me now?"

Was that what it seemed like? Brad panicked for the split second it took him to notice the smile lingering at the corners of Colin's lips. "I had to make sure you didn't flee the country in terror," he replied in as flat a tone as he could manage.

"No terror." Colin closed the door of his locker, leaned against it, and crossed his arms over his chest. He smelled faintly of alcohol. He'd been drinking. And hadn't shaved. "Just work. Lots of work."

Brad didn't steal a glance at Colin's pecs flexing. Nope. "So much work you couldn't return one of my calls? Why don't you just admit it? You had fun with Becca, but aren't interested in more. And that's okay." He meant it, even though he really wished that wasn't the case. "Just don't be a prick about it. Don't drop off the face of the earth. We didn't mean to freak you out. I swear we won't even mention it again. Just…"

Just what? Just still be his friend? He wasn't in high school any more. Still… "Friends?" He took a step back and held out his hand. It wasn't exactly a smooth move, but he needed the reassurance.

Colin didn't reach for his hand. If anything, his posture seemed more guarded, his shoulders folded inward, his chin low. "I told you we're fine."

Brad was grateful the next round of classes started in a few minutes and the changing rooms were swiftly emptying, because he wouldn't be civil for much longer.

He waited until the last of the gym-goers was out the door, and then slammed his palm on the locker, next to Colin's head. "We're not fine. *Fuck* fine." He liked the way the profanity tasted. It filled the mouth every time. He'd been using it more since he got with Becca, and he couldn't believe he'd avoided it for so many years.

"You're freaked out or pissed off, or something, and it's my fault. I should have backed down when you said you wouldn't do it, but all your excuses had to do with how I'd react. I thought you were trying to protect me. When I saw how into Becca you were once clothes were off, I thought you enjoyed it. I didn't—"

"I did enjoy it." The words were whispered. "It was fucking awesome. I haven't managed to think of anything else for the past three days. I keep revisiting that scene in my head. I've jerked off to it more times than I can count." He rubbed his face, avoiding Brad's gaze.

This was going a completely different way than Brad had expected. A much better way. "Then join us on Saturday."

"No."

Brad rolled his shoulders. Colin could be infuriating when he was like this. He wouldn't tell Brad what the matter was, even though there was obviously something wrong. Unluckily for Colin, Brad wasn't used to losing arguments in or out of court. "What is it? Talk to me. Is it that we went about it so sneakily? I told you why we did it. I promise everything will be straight forward now on."

Colin snorted. "Now on? You mean on Saturday? When I'm to be Becca's present?" His words were laced with distaste.

"Is that your problem? You think we see you as a thing? A sex toy?" Brad couldn't help raising his voice and was glad there were no spectators. "We'd have used a vibrator, if that was the case, Colin. I want her to have that experience, and I want to share it with you. If you're not cool with it, if you're upset for whatever reason—"

Colin glared. "I already told you I had fun. No harm, no foul. I'm just busy on Saturday, but I'm fine. Honest."

Brad leaned in closer. "Then why is your pulse jumping in your throat? Tell me the truth."

Colin frowned. He opened his mouth, then closed it again and huffed. By the time he finally spoke, he looked pained. "Okay. Here's some truth for you, but remember I didn't want to say anything. I loved fucking Becca."

"Yeah, well, that was the point."

Colin shook his head. "You don't get it. I loved being with her. Inside her. But it's more than that. I think of her more than I should. I like talking to her, and I actually care what she has to say." He gave Brad a pleading look. "I can't remember the last time I… If I touch her again, if I keep seeing her like that, I won't be able to handle it. It won't just be fucking."

Brad should be jealous. A few months ago, with another girl, he'd have been upset, but a few months ago he wouldn't have dreamed of doing half the things he did with Becca.

Colin got in his face. "Say something. Yell at me. I'm falling for your girl, damn it." He sounded close to breaking down. "Tell me I'm filthy. That I should keep my distance. Tell me you never want to see me again."

Brad was the one who insisted Colin have sex with Becca. Brad orchestrated the ruse that gave Becca the time to chip away at Colin's defenses, and to his surprise, he wasn't bothered at all by what he was hearing. All he could think was that he didn't want Colin hurting.

"Saturday doesn't have to be a one-time thing." Brad tried to pour more meaning into his tone than his words conveyed. "Becca and I have talked about it. We can keep having fun. All three of us."

Colin grabbed his shirt in both fists and shook him. "This isn't about having fun. This isn't about doing it like bunnies. I'm not your fuck toy. I can't check my feelings at the door and leave the two of you in each other's arms at the end of the night."

"That's not what we're asking," Brad said. Wasn't it? And when did he and Becca decide on wanting anything more than an extra body in their bed on occasion? Colin made sense, and Brad had to respect his friend's wishes. "I get it, though," he said. "I won't pressure you into joining us this Saturday. Becca will understand. Subject is closed." He didn't know how he managed to be so calm, when his heart hammered in his chest.

The subject was apparently not closed for Colin. "I'm afraid, man. You were right. I'm scared I'll fall for her and lose you. That I'll cost you one another. Aren't you?"

Brad probably should be. Colin was a charismatic asshole, and even though Brad suspected his own feelings for Becca were returned, relationships ended all the time. She might eventually choose Colin over him, and then he'd have no one. But first he had to have them both. He could figure things out later.

"No," he said. "I'm not. You talk about living life to the fullest, but you chicken out when it gets real. Even if feelings do develop, even if things get out of hand, I'm ready for anything. I have Becca, and maybe we'll find someone else to join us." The last bit was added out of spite. He wanted to piss Colin off. Maybe that would take his own mind off why he was trying to convince his friend it was okay to fall for his girlfriend.

"What I feel is wrong." Colin still held on to Brad's shirt.

"Not if it doesn't hurt anyone."

"It can hurt me," Colin said through gritted teeth.

"I won't let it." Again Brad made a promise he didn't fully understand. "If you fall for her, and she falls for you… maybe she won't have to choose." Where had that come from? He and Becca had invited Colin to their bed, not their relationship.

Colin's eyes held confusion and something else. Hope? Whatever it was, it vanished as swiftly as it had appeared. "Please let it go. This isn't good for any of us. What happened — I shouldn't have done it."

He regretted one of the best nights of Brad's life.

Ice water poured through Brad's veins. "I see. Okay." He slapped Colin's hands away, and turned to leave.

"I said I'd tell you the truth, so" — Colin took a sharp breath — "it's not just about Becca. I can't do this with you. "

Brad faced him again. Studied his drawn face through narrowed eyes. Did Colin mean he wanted Becca to himself, or…

"If I keep seeing you naked, so close to me, eventually looking won't be enough. I'll slip, and I'll touch you. And you'll be disgusted by me."

Brad could hear the unspoken 'too.' Colin had told him about his fallout with his brother, who'd waited until their father was hospitalized to spew bile at Colin for his sexual preferences. "I'm not Alan, Colin."

Colin let out a forced laugh. "Oh, believe me, I know. I never wanted to fuck my brother."

And there it was, out in the open. The one word that changed it all.

Fuck.

Colin wanted to fuck him.

And Brad was actually wondering how that would feel. Who'd be plowing whose ass? Would it hurt?

"Say something," Colin said.

Wasn't it funny how Brad had bitched that Colin didn't talk to him, and now he was the one at a loss for words?

"Fuck. Talk to me, Brad."

There was that word again. Before he even realized he was doing it, Brad grabbed Colin from the back of his neck and smashed his lips to Colin's.

Colin dug his fingers into Brad's shoulders, but made no effort to pull away. He did nothing at first—just stood stock still, while Brad probed at his lips with his tongue. Then, as if his resistance melted away, he slid his large palms up to cup Brad's face and sucked on Brad's tongue. He nipped at Brad's lower lip, gently at first, then bit harder.

Brad growled. He drove Colin backward without breaking the kiss, until Colin was sandwiched between Brad's body and the row of lockers, one of Brad's thighs wedged between Colin's legs. Colin's erection felt warm through Brad's jeans. The towel must have slipped away.

Brad wanted to look down, but he was too busy being lost in Colin's mouth. His lips weren't as smooth as Brad was used to, and his stubble scratched, but his mouth felt every bit as inviting as Becca's.

Becca. Shit. Brad couldn't be doing this. He had a girlfriend.

He wasn't gay.

Couldn't be kissing Colin—and liking it.

Shit.

Fuck.

Brad pulled away, shaking his head. He couldn't look at Colin, or he might end up losing himself in another kiss. "I'm sorry. I shouldn't have done that." He turned and fled.

Colin's voice still caught up with him. "Tell me again nobody gets hurt."

Chapter Fourteen

Brad should talk to Becca. She wasn't easily shocked and often knew what he wanted before he did. Maybe she'd help him clear his head, or even indulge him, like he did her. She might insist he shouldn't deny himself his wants. Talk to Colin. The three of them could have fun in combinations other than what Brad initially planned for Saturday.

Of course, she might not be half as understanding as he hoped. She might leave him. And the way he'd run out on Colin, Colin probably wouldn't want anything more to do with him either.

How had he messed up this way? Why did he have to kiss Colin like that?

He'd do it again in a heartbeat.

His phone buzzed again. The prolonged vibration meant a call. He glanced at the screen. Becca's smiling face looked up at him. He'd taken this pic just before she'd gone down on him in a parking lot.

His cock stirred again—not that his erection had abated completely since his lips had found Colin's.

He smacked the wheel and put the call on speaker. "Hey, babe."

"Hello, Bradley."

His erection problem was instantly resolved by his mother's dry voice. Shit. She was with Becca.

"Mother. How may I help you?"

"You may answer your phone when I repeatedly try to reach you. We had an appointment today, which you missed."

He grimaced. "I'm sorry. Something came up. I thought Sarah explained."

Becca should be at work. Even if she forgave him for kissing a guy, she'd kill him for being the reason his mother dropped in on her. While she painted the same apartment she and Colin had fucked in on Friday.

Brad's life was way too complicated.

"Something always seems to come up lately." Her tone went impossibly more frigid. "I blame it on the company you keep."

She meant Becca. She'd disliked her instantly when the two met during one of his mother's surprise visits at his place. Brad went from defensive to pissed-off in no time. "You better get used to that company, Mother. I plan on keeping her around for a long time."

She gave a delicate snort. Everything the woman did came off as delicate, even though she was one of the hardest people he knew. It was all part of the deception that for years had convinced him she was always right.

"We'll see about that," she said.

Brad honked at someone trying to overtake him, and swerved left to get out of traffic. He had to get to Becca before his mother did more damage than his upcoming confession would. "Was there a reason for this phone call, other to point out everything that's wrong with my life?" He didn't try to hide his irritation.

"There was, indeed. I've had an offer to sell the company. I wanted to do you the courtesy of informing you in person, but since you couldn't keep our appointment" — she sighed — "I guess this will have to suffice. I'll need you to prepare a full presentation on the company's growth the past three years, first thing Wednesday morning."

"You're going ahead with the sale?" His father had built the company. It was the reason he'd been absent most of Brad's childhood. Brad wouldn't let her see how much he hated the idea of selling, but she knew.

"I'm certainly considering it."

Punishment. She was taking the company from him, as punishment for Becca. "Who's the buyer?" he asked, unable to think of anything else to say.

His mother either didn't hear him or decided to ignore his question. Her voice sounded far from the receiver. "Here you are, Rebecca. I'm sure my son will need some consoling now. That *is* what you're good at, I suppose."

"Mother." His voice was a growl, but the line went dead. Becca could handle his mother, but she shouldn't have to, damn it. His family. His problem.

He'd warned his mother not to make him choose, but she was too stubborn to just let things go. He stepped on the gas and took a narrow right turn. He was minutes from the building Becca worked on. If he got there before his mother left, she would get a long-overdue earful.

He parked just as his mother's car peeled off the curve. His choices were to either go after her, or run to Becca and do some damage control. As much as he itched to tell his mother exactly what he thought of her, Becca was a priority. And maybe losing the company would be a good thing. He could return to practicing law, and his mother would lose the final dregs of her hold on him.

He locked the car and took the stairs up two at a time. The third floor felt miles away, and his imagination ran rampant. Becca wouldn't be there. She'd have finally realized he was too much trouble. His mother could have threatened her. Tried to buy her off. Becca wasn't interested in his money, but if she thought they had no future together, she might take the way out.

He had to get a grip. This was his life, not a soap opera, and even if Lorena Miller went around buying people, Becca wasn't for sale.

He stormed inside the apartment, and his heart skipped a beat when he didn't see Becca in the living room. "Becca? Baby?"

Nothing. She couldn't have just up and left without a word. Maybe she was in the bathroom. Or downstairs grabbing a snack. To his surprise, he found her painting the second bedroom, a beer bottle in her left hand.

"You okay?" he asked.

When she didn't answer, he noticed her earphones. She was listening to music.

"Becca," he said louder.

She snapped her head his way and smiled when she saw him. "Hi, you."

"Are you okay?"

"Sure." She pulled out the earphones, and her hair moved off her left cheek, to reveal a vivid blush from her chin to the corner of her eye.

No. Not a blush. "She slapped you?" Brad saw red. He clenched his fists and gritted his teeth, to bite back the bile he felt for his mother.

"She slapped me *first*."

An incredulous chuckle escaped him. "You slapped my mother?" He wished he'd witnessed that. His mother was used to trampling all over people, but Becca had given her a taste of her own medicine. Not even the part of him that harbored his leftover Catholic guilt had a problem with that.

The smile fell from Becca's lips. "As I said, she started it. And she continued it with some lovely words about my weight and sexual proclivities."

"Fuck." He punched the wall, and felt like an idiot when his knuckles came away scraped and coated with pale blue paint. "That woman drives me nuts."

"I know she's your mother, but she's a horrible person. Really horrible." Her façade cracked, and he saw the pain and insecurity beneath it. Her beautiful eyes were red rimmed, and her lower lip trembled. "I mean, I held my own, but—"

He closed the distance between them and wrapped her in his arms. In her flats, she was a foot shorter than his six-foot-four, and despite her curves, felt small against him. She buried her face in his chest, and though she made no sound, he felt her tears soaking his shirt.

"She's beyond horrible, but whatever her issue, it's with me. You're perfect the way you are. Don't let her make you doubt yourself. You're gorgeous and smart and" — fuck it; he wouldn't wait any longer — "I love you."

"I called her a bitch. I called your mom a bitch. I'm so sorry." Her voice was muffled. Had she heard him?

It didn't matter. He'd say it again, when she was happy, and she'd hear him then. "She deserved worse. I'm sorry I wasn't here. I should have dealt with her, but I thought she'd eventually cool down."

"So you don't hate me?"

"No, but I'll have to fire you."

"Are you serious?" She looked up at him, eyes wide as saucers.

"No."

She smacked his shoulder lightly. "I don't know what's better. Your timing or your sense of humor."

He tangled his fingers in her hair, and laid a gentle kiss on her lips. "We may both lose our jobs."

"I know."

And that was much more important than his confession about what happened with Colin. He didn't need to burden her with his inner turmoil, when her livelihood was at stake.

And maybe he was kind of a wuss and looking for any excuse to put off owning up to what he'd done.

"Did Colin call?" she asked.

"He texted that we're all right, and I dropped by the gym to talk to him."

"And?"

And Brad had kissed him. "I'll tell you all about it tonight, if I wrap up this stupid presentation early."

She studied his face for a moment and then nodded. "Go. Get things done, so you can come by later." She licked his lower lip, before pulling it between her teeth.

The woman was sex on legs, but also smart, compassionate, and funny. Brad thanked his lucky stars for her once more. Just seeing her for a minute, a kiss, and things already seemed less bleak. Of course he still had to tell her about the other kiss, but he'd broach the subject tonight and hope for the best.

"And you finish up here and go home. Ms. Thing will be one pissed-off pussy, if you leave her alone one more evening."

Becca laughed that throaty laugh of hers that made him want to rip off her clothes. "You're good with pussies," she said. "I bet you can calm her down."

He hated to leave her, especially when she slid his hand between her legs. "Becca, I need to work," he said with a groan.

"I know, but I don't have to like it."

"I'm sorry I won't be able to give you that bath." Or lick whipped cream off her naked body. "But I promise to get you all nice and dirty first chance I get."

"It's okay. It's not your fault. Come over whenever you're done? I hate sleeping alone."

He nodded. He loved that she craved his company as much as he did hers. "It'll be late."

She shrugged, kissed him, and smacked his ass. "Off you go. See you tonight."

It was already tonight, and all he wanted was to join her in bed, but he said goodbye and left with a heavy heart and more promises to make it up to her.

Chapter Fifteen

Brad called his CFO from the car, and the man returned to the office and provided Brad with complete reports on the company's finances and liquidity, but it was up to Brad to prepare the presentation his mother had requested.

Ordered. The woman didn't do requests.

Brad really didn't want to do this, but it was his job, and he wouldn't let his mother see how it hurt him to comply with her wishes.

He pinched the bridge of his nose. The artificial lighting gave him a migraine. Or maybe his computer screen was to blame. He'd been looking at it for three hours now.

Nah. The only one to blame was his mother, with her holier-than-thou attitude and her insistence to take away everything that made him happy.

On Brad's sixth birthday, his father gave him a Golden Retriever puppy. Brad's mother had looked at the dog like it was the scourge of the earth and declared it was to be entirely Brad's responsibility — as if anyone would trust *her* with a living being. Brad's nanny offered to walk the pup, but his mother wouldn't have it. Brad would have to care for it on his own, or lose it.

The first time the puppy had an accident in the house, Brad's mother gave it to their next-door neighbor. Brad supposed he ought to feel grateful she didn't have it put down.

The pattern hadn't been broken since. Every time Brad found something or someone that made him happy, his mother made sure to show him how temporary everything was. She'd done it with his first girlfriend, whom his mother forced to admit she wasn't a virgin and then threatened with the fires of hell, if she got Brad into trouble before he'd finished college.

Losing his first love might have stung at the time, but what he lamented the most was the last thing his mother took from him. He loved practicing law, but his mother wanted him to take on the family business. If he didn't, she'd close it down, and people he grew up around would lose their job.

Once he decided abstinence wasn't for him, Brad made sure to keep his relationships from his mother. Still, he'd come to believe her version of the natural order of things—that he wasn't supposed to be happy. And then Becca crashed through his illusions and brought down the barriers his mother had helped build around him.

He remembered lying next to her that first night, staring at her ceiling and wondering how on earth he'd got to thirty six without knowing sex could be this incredible. Midnight had come and gone hours ago.

"I should be going," he'd said.

Becca had laughed. "You *shouldn't* do anything. Your life is your own. Do you *want* to go home?"

He hadn't. He'd stayed at her place, and they hadn't slept a wink.

He wanted to be with her now, instead of preparing reports. The spreadsheet blurred in front of him.

His desk phone rang, and he jumped at the distraction. Other than his CFO and his mother, Becca was the only one who knew where he was at this hour. "Hello?"

"Becca told me you'd be there." Colin's crisp tone sent a shiver down Brad's spine.

"You talked to Becca?"

"Only to ask for you, when she answered your cell phone."

His cell phone? "Must have dropped it when" — when he went to tell her he kissed Colin, but chickened out — "I went to see her."

"I'm coming up."

"What?"

"I'm downstairs. Coming up. Buzz me in. Got beer."

Brad could say he was busy, that they'd talk some other time, but even if beer weren't the great incentive it was, he couldn't brush Colin off. Not after Brad ran out on him at the gym.

He pressed the buzzer and sat waiting. The familiar chime of the elevator doors opening reached his ears, and moments later Colin pushed his door open.

"You should be the one bringing me a peace offering," Colin said, "but Becca said you're swamped, so—"

"So you thought you'd come bug me." Falling into the familiar banter was easy. As long as they steered clear of dangerous subjects, they'd be fine.

"What are friends for?" Colin sprawled on the leather sofa, took two bottles of beer out of the bag he held, and propped them on the coffee table. His smile didn't reach his dark-blue eyes.

Brad got up from his chair and joined him on the couch, leaving as much distance between them as the wide two-seater allowed. "I was about to order Chinese from the only decent place delivering at this hour."

"Don't feel like Chinese." Colin's gaze said he was starving, and Brad felt a lump form in his throat. So much for keeping it safe.

"So…" Brad couldn't fathom how to finish that sentence.

"You kissed me."

No preamble, then. No time for him to come up with something to talk about that had nothing to do with the two of them. "I did." He swallowed, but the knot was still there.

"And then you took off."

"Yes."

"I waited for you to call with some lame excuse, but you didn't."

Brad sucked in a deep breath. He didn't care about many people and couldn't afford to lose the ones he loved. Colin was still his best friend. Brad could be straight with him. Well, not exactly. He could be honest, in any case. "I probably would have, but I didn't get to. My mother called to tell me she wants to sell Miller Co., and I'm to help her create a presentation that shows how marketable we are."

"Huh. I didn't see that coming. I was expecting something more like you went to see Becca and were too busy fucking her to give me a second thought."

Brad winced, but tried to keep his voice light. "Yeah, wish that were the case."

Colin folded a leg under him and turned to face him fully. "Is she going to go through with the sale?"

"Your guess is as good as mine." Brad gave a one-shoulder shrug.

"That sucks."

"Yeah."

"Are you staying on, if she does?"

"No clue."

"What about Becca?"

Brad shook his head. "I really don't know. It will all depend on the new owner, but we should both start looking."

"I can help. We work with construction companies and interior designers. I can put in a good word about either of you. I'll start making some calls in the morning."

"Thanks, man." Brad squeezed Colin's leg. He left his touch linger, until the muscle contracted under his touch. "I think I may try being a lawyer again. I was better at it than I am at this."

"Why did you kiss me?" Like a dog with a bone, this one.

Brad hung his head. "I'm sorry."

"Why?"

"I shouldn't have. I'm with Becca, and I didn't tell her about it. I will. Tomorrow."

"Tell her what?" Colin tilted his head, until his gaze found Brad's.

"About the kiss."

"You don't have to. Nothing happened."

The day had taken its toll on Brad, but now exhaustion was giving its place to irritation. He turned to glare at Colin. "Something fucking happened. I kissed you."

"We're talking in circles. If you didn't want to kiss me and don't plan on doing it again, there's no reason to strain your relationship with Becca." Colin searched Brad's face.

"I didn't mean to kiss you—"

"Well, there you go then." Colin arched an eyebrow and gave Brad one of his devil-may-care smirks.

"—but I don't know if I'd do it again." The admission hurt Brad's ears, but he had to be true to himself and to Colin.

"Let's find out." Colin's voice was gruffer, and Brad felt a tightening in his groin.

"How?" Was he crazy? He should put a stop to this now. Nothing more could or should happen until he talked to Becca. He wasn't even sure he wanted to find out what he'd do, given another chance to taste Colin's lips.

He was still thinking about it, when Colin fisted one hand in his shirt and pulled him closer. Their faces were a hairsbreadth apart. Colin had shaved since the gym. Pity. He looked even better when he let himself go a little scruffy.

Brad licked his lips. He should pull away. Push Colin away. Throw him out of the office and get back to work.

Instead, he rubbed his cheek against Colin's.

"Kiss me." Colin's whispered command cracked through the silence in the room.

"I can't."

"Then tell me you don't want to, and I'll let it go."

Brad couldn't do that, either. Colin's breath in his ear, his cheek cool against Brad's heated skin, stole away all but the last dregs of Brad's reason. Instinct and desire reigned over common sense. He inhaled deeply, letting the scent of Colin's body wash and deo fill his nostrils. Such a male scent, nothing like Becca's flowery perfumes, and yet now it made Brad's body react the same way.

His lips tingled, and his nerve endings felt raw with desire. His cock strained against his slacks. What the hell had he started? How was he going to tame this new need that tore him up inside? What was he risking, if he gave in?

"Tell me you don't want to kiss me." Any reluctance, any uncertainty Colin had exhibited earlier was gone. He was the master of the game, like usual, and Brad was tempted to turn him down just to throw him off his high horse. He might have, if Colin's warm hand wasn't pressing down on his thigh, burning him.

"Shut up." Brad's voice sounded horse to his own ears.

"Tell me."

If Colin asked one more time, Brad would kiss him, and if their lips met again, there was no telling where this would end. But it couldn't even start unless he talked to Becca. "Becca—"

"She's already slept with me, if that's all that's holding you back. If it's not, tell me you don't want to kiss me."

"Shut the fuck up, Colin."

"Make me."

"Shit." Brad dug his fingers at the base of Colin's skull and attacked his lips with a ferociousness he didn't know he had in him. He'd never kissed anyone this way. Never felt the need to. But it was different with Colin. The kiss was as natural as an extension of their verbal sparring and just as merciless. Teeth clashed together, and tongues fought for dominance. He bit on Colin's lower lip. His jaw. Then his lip again.

It was one hell of a kiss, and when Colin pulled away, Brad wanted more. He didn't say so. Didn't say anything. Just sat there, watching bewildered as Colin trailed his tongue across his front teeth.

Silence. What to say now? Was there some protocol for how to go about making small talk, after locking lips with his best friend?

Colin probably had the same issue, because he didn't talk either. Just studied him, brow furrowed. Was something wrong? Something other than the obvious? Maybe he felt no chemistry after all. That would solve his problems. If Colin no longer wanted him, he wouldn't have a problem with the three way. And if Colin was off the table, Brad didn't have to worry about his own feelings.

He should be relieved.

It felt like a kick to the balls, but it was for the best.

Brad was trying to come up with something sarcastic and cool to say, when Colin nodded to himself and went down on his knees in the narrow space between the sofa and the coffee table.

"What are you doing?" Brad sputtered.

Colin crawled between Brad's legs, grabbed Brad's belt, and tugged. When Brad dug his loafers into the plush carpet to stay in place, Colin just pulled harder until Brad's ass was on the edge of the cushion.

"Colin…"

Colin didn't seem to hear. He pursed his lips, his focus not shifting from his work, as he undid Brad's buckle. Leaving the belt in the loops, he popped the button and lowered the zipper of Brad's slacks.

Brad tried to grasp the cushion, to anchor himself. The creaking of leather reminded him he should be objecting — maybe batting Colin's hands away — not trying to find purchase. "Are you drunk?" he asked.

"Not enough. I still care whether you'll speak to me tomorrow, but I've put this off way too long." Colin closed his fist around Brad's cock and pulled it out of his pants.

Brad hissed. He should have worn boxer shorts. Another layer of clothing might have delayed Colin enough for Brad's mind to start working again.

"This was what I meant to do first time we went out for beers." Colin slid his hand down to Brad's balls and up again. "I wasn't supposed to like you. I didn't want to be your friend. I wanted to fuck you."

What was he saying? He didn't to be Brad's friend? If he'd been playing the long game, it was a pretty darn long one, since he'd never made a move in six years. Brad's heart and brain did somersaults, but his cock didn't mind the attention one bit. It strained and throbbed with every stroke.

"I'm not into sucking cock." Colin's voice was matter of fact. "I prefer being on the receiving end. But I've been thinking of this since Friday. I wanted to see you pull on your dick for me, and I wanted to taste you."

Brad groaned. "Colin, what are you doing?"

"If you haven't figured it out by now, I don't know how you made it through law school."

Every muscle in Brad's body was tense, and he wanted nothing more than to pump his hips and force his shaft down Colin's throat, but this wasn't just a kiss. "We do this, and everything changes."

"Maybe it's time for some change." Colin's lips hovered over the head of Brad's cock, but didn't make contact.

If Brad as much as inhaled sharply, he'd bump against the sensual mouth. He tried to keep his breathing shallow. "I don't want to mess things up."

"Do I stop?"

Yes. He should stop. They should agree they had one too many beers, and avoid each other for a few days until they could put this behind them. While they still could put it behind them.

Brad closed his eyes and threw an arm over his face. "No." The whispered word had barely left his lips, when Colin's warm mouth closed around him.

Chapter Sixteen

Brad hummed. He wanted to curse, call out Colin's name, do something, but his pleasure sapped his will. He grabbed onto his seat, nails wounding the leather. Colin sucked like a fucking Hoover.

One hard yank, and Brad's pants slipped down his legs. He let his knees fall open further, and sucked air through clenched teeth when Colin closed a hand over his sac and tugged while sliding his mouth up Brad's cock.

"God…"

Colin laughed around Brad's shaft, the vibrations sending jolts of pleasure to Brad's balls.

His mother would have a stroke, if she found out Brad called His name while Colin went down on him.

Colin's teeth grazed the underside of Brad's cock, and Brad shuddered. He wanted to look. Wanted to see Colin's blue eyes watching him, as Brad's length disappeared between his lips, but that might be awkward.

That might be awkward? He chuckled. He fought with his shame and opened his eyes. As he'd expected, Colin's gaze was on him.

Brad's balls twitched. He was close, but didn't want to give in yet. Colin's mouth was amazing, and that he wasn't afraid to be rough heightened Brad's pleasure.

Colin pulled back, and Brad's dick came out with a wet plop. Brad was bewildered. Why was he stopping? Fuck, he should have let himself come already.

Colin smirked and spat saliva on his index and middle finger.

Brad felt the blood rush out of his head. He wasn't ready for that. Becca had tried to sneak her pinky in his ass once, and he'd lost his erection and his head. And Becca's fingers weren't nearly as large as Colin's were.

"I don't think—"

"I'll stop the minute you tell me to." Colin's mouth was back on Brad's cock, sucking and licking, while he massaged Brad's balls.

Brad couldn't relax completely into the sensations, especially when he felt one finger brush his asshole. He clenched his ass, and Colin sucked harder, flicking his tongue over the glans.

The finger became more persistent, prodding and rubbing, until Brad pushed back against it.

Colin let go of Brad's cock long enough to say, "That's it. Now one more. You'll see, you'll love it."

Brad seriously doubted it, but he did love Colin's tongue on his balls and then his perineum. *Oh.* The sneaky bastard was trying to add more saliva so he could…

More pressure, and Brad felt more stretched than he ever cared to be. "Colin—"

"Almost there. Take a deep breath." Colin gulped Brad's cock down again and swallowed until the bell end touched the back of his throat.

This was good. This was very good. Brad almost said so, when Colin forced his fingers in further. Brad's eyes teared up.

"They're in up to the first knuckle," Colin said. Why was he talking instead of blowing him? "If you get past the second, it's pure bliss."

Second? Knuckle? Panic made Brad light headed. Colin was going deeper?

He was, and none too gently.

Colin bit lightly on Brad's cockhead and pushed harder than before.

Brad's asshole burned at the intrusion. "Fuck." Too much. For the first time since Colin knelt in front of him, Brad touched him. He tried to grasp Colin's hair, as he would Becca's, but Colin wasn't Becca. No mane to hold on to, while Brad fucked his mouth. He palmed the back of Colin's head instead, and drove deeper. The man had no gag reflex. Thank fu—

Colin slid his fingers out of Brad's ass and slammed them back inside. And again. Faster. Harder. He sucked Brad's cock and fingered Brad's ass until Brad couldn't tell pleasure from pain.

Brad rolled his head on his shoulders, shut his eyes again, and pumped his hips as fast as he could.

Colin's fingers found something inside that made Brad want to laugh and cry at the same time. It still hurt, but pain and pleasure were a blur, making his head light and his movements jerky.

He was close, and there was no delaying it this time. "I'm coming."

Instead of pulling away, Colin sucked harder. His fingers thrust inside Brad faster.

Brad wanted to say something more, but his balls tightened, and his cum spurted down Colin's throat for what felt like forever.

Colin kept on sucking, until he'd swallowed every drop.

Still in a haze, Brad wondered again about protocol. Did he pull Colin up and kiss him, like he would Becca? Was he supposed to return the favor? He was less opposed to the idea than he'd have been this morning, but it was still too much.

His ass was sore, but he felt bereft when Colin withdrew his fingers.

The shame he should feel wasn't there, and he didn't know how to deal without it. He had to say something. Had to at least look at Colin and smile. Show him what just happened was fucking awesome.

Colin gazed up at him, his face blank.

Brad really had to come up with something *now*. The silence stretched. Covering them. Freaking him out. And Colin watched him, blue eyes darkening.

Every minute Brad said nothing made speaking even harder, until he could feel the awkwardness pressing down on his chest.

Colin wiped his mouth with his thumb and then sucked on the tip. "So that happened." He sounded as disinterested as he looked. Brad knew him better than that. Colin wouldn't have thrown away their friendship for a blow job.

Though he was very convincing, if he wanted to show how little this meant to him.

He needed to finish his presentation and come clean to Becca before he could tackle his newfound and completely baffling feelings for Colin. "I… have to work." Shit. Wrong thing to say. He'd meant it as an explanation—no, as an excuse for not returning the favor. For putting off the discussion they should have.

Colin's jaw tightened. He nodded. "Yeah. I'll go."

"Unless you wanna stay and eat? We could still get something." Brad should have already ordered. Then he'd have stuffed his mouth with pork rolls, instead of with his foot.

Colin stood, shaking his head. "I'm good. 'Sides, you got to work." Could he sound any snarkier?

"Can I call you tomorrow?" What was wrong? Why was this so uncomfortable? Why couldn't Brad look his best friend in the eye? Oh, right. *Because he'd shot his load down his best friend's throat.*

"Sure. We'll go out for coffee and talk about chicks. Maybe discuss how we'll both fuck your girlfriend on Saturday."

"Colin, don't be like that."

"Like what?" Colin's eyes were tight, when Brad finally met his gaze.

"You know what I mean." Brad tried to put his thoughts in order, but his brain seemed to have leaked out of his cock. He tried. "What just happened—"

"The blow job I gave you?"

"Yes. That."

"Let me guess. It can't happen again."

128

"Will you fucking let me speak?" Brad jumped up, and his cock brushed Colin's hip. He shouldn't be this aware of Colin's body.

He shouldn't be this attracted to him.

He shouldn't have allowed things to get this far.

But he'd fucking loved it.

Pity he couldn't say so in a coherent manner.

"Still waiting." Colin crossed his arms. His forearms pressed against Brad's chest, nearly making him lose his balance.

"I can't talk about this right now. I didn't expect it, and I didn't expect to like it, and I can't wrap my mind around it. This isn't the right time."

"Message received." Colin sidestepped him and turned toward the door.

"Colin, stop."

Colin didn't turn around. "Too late for that now."

Brad should chase after him, but his trousers were still pooled around his ankles, his squeaky clean cock hanging limp, and his brain was all jumbled up and useless. He stood there, feeling miserable, long after the door had closed behind Colin.

He'd messed everything up. Becca was going to drop him as soon as he told her what happened. He loved her too much to keep it from her. Confessing he kissed Colin might have been forgiven, but he'd let Colin suck him off, and he was pretty sure that counted as cheating.

He could pretend it meant nothing, but he knew better. It meant he and Colin couldn't get back to being buddies. It meant Brad had cheated. It meant he wasn't the man he thought he was, or who he wanted to be.

As for it happening again… If all Colin had wanted since he met Brad was to fuck him, he'd gotten close to getting his wish. Maybe he'd have taken things further if Brad had shown more enthusiasm after the blowjob. Maybe Colin's behavior the past few days had been nothing but a show, to get Brad to this very moment. He might make another move soon. Would Brad stop him then?

The shame finally came. Shame that he thought so little of a man who'd been his best friend for years. At least Colin had gone after what he wanted, unlike Brad, who used his denial as a shield.

Brad seriously doubted he could work more tonight. All he wanted was to go to Becca, sink inside her body, and let her moans drown out the confusion and guilt eating at him.

Too soon. Colin's saliva wasn't even dry on Brad's cock.

Fuck.

No girlfriend. No best friend. Soon no company, either.

Brad had lost everything.

And he still felt the afterglow of the best blow job he'd ever had.

He tucked in his dick and zipped up, not bothering with the button or his belt. He went to his desk and made himself comfortable in his chair. If he'd be spending the night, he might as well have lumbar support. The heap of papers in front of him mocked him. He moved the mouse around and waited for the screen to light up. The presentation awaited, and it was the only thing in his life right now that he knew what to do with.

When he sorted it out, he'd hand it to his mother and let her do as she pleased with it and with the company. He might feel responsible for the people who worked there, but he didn't belong there.

He'd take a sick day or ten, go home alone—he'd better get used to being alone, anyway—and figure out where he stood on tonight's events. Then he'd wait for his balls to drop, so he could face Becca and own up to every single thought and feeling he'd had since Friday. Correction—every single thought, feeling, and *experience* he'd had since then.

He'd beg her for forgiveness, and he'd do the same with Colin until they both accepted his apologies.

He had to fix things.

Starting with his relationship with his mother.

He cracked his knuckles and rolled up his sleeves.

This presentation would blow her mind.

Becca

Chapter Seventeen

Becca was drowning.

Heavy. Pressure. She gasped. Something pressed down on her. She couldn't suck in a breath.

She opened her eyes, and swatted at the grey Persian cat sitting on her chest. "Ms. Thing, how many times do I have to tell you my boobs are not your pillows?"

Ms. Thing slinked down by Becca's thigh, and gave her a most disinterested feline stretch.

Becca turned to look at her alarm clock. Eight sixteen. In the morning. Brad hadn't come home all night. Poor man would be exhausted by the time he was done with the financial report Lorena demanded.

His mother could be such a bitch some times. Becca didn't really regret calling her that to her face, but she hated adding to Brad's tension. Brad had assured her his mother disapproved of everything he liked, and would cause him trouble even if he wasn't dating Becca. Becca wasn't sure about that. After all, Lorena had told her she'd leave the company in Brad's hands, if Becca broke up with him.

"I've put too much into Miller Co. to see a fat little gold-digger get her filthy paws on it," Lorena had said.

"God, you're a bitch," Becca had replied.

Lorena had slapped her.

And then Becca had returned the favor.

Brad's all-nighter was because of Becca, and she knew it. She'd make it up to him tonight, and while she was at it, she'd tell him about his mother's offer. Last night she didn't want him to worry about her wounded pride when he had so much work ahead of him, but they'd have to talk about it. Only fair he get the choice about his future.

And wasn't that a downer of a wake-up thought?

At the insistent meowing of Ms. Thing, Becca slipped out of bed. She didn't have to go in for work today. She'd finished painting the last apartment, and she wasn't supposed to start on the next Miller Co. contract till Monday. Assuming she was still with Miller Co. till then.

She stretched and rolled her head. She'd make the most of her free morning. Have a big breakfast, do her nails... Maybe go buy that shoulder bag she'd been drooling over for two months now.

She could call Amanda, and have a girls' day.

Becca played with the idea just long enough to admit she liked having some time to herself. Brad was all kinds of amazing, and completely worth giving up her old ways, but she missed her peace and quiet some days.

She missed other things too, but it seemed she'd found the perfect workaround for that.

Becca smiled to herself as she pulled on a pair of sweatpants and one of the t-shirts Brad had left at her place. She loved smelling him on her.

When she and Brad had talked about fantasies, she hadn't expected him to be open to bringing someone else into their bed, but it had worked out swimmingly—if she ignored the part where Colin freaked out and disappeared afterwards.

Insecurities she'd long ago tried to get rid of gnawed at her. Brad assumed Colin freaked out because he'd slept with Brad's girlfriend, but maybe that wasn't it. Maybe he just never wanted to fuck her, and had only done so as a favor to Brad. The idea of touching her again might be a turnoff. She remembered his dark blue eyes pining her in place as he thrust inside her. There was nothing but lust and wonder in his gaze. Nothing to indicate he wasn't there on his own free will. He'd wanted to fuck her.

That was it, wasn't it? All the pretty words he'd said were just words. He'd pretended to fight against his desire for her because it wasn't just skin deep, because he was a master at sweet talking women into sleeping with him. The man had game; there was no denying that. The lingering looks and touches, and the softness he'd let her glimpse under the gorgeous surface were nothing more than his usual spiel for closing the deal.

"Decide, woman," she muttered to herself. "Either he never wanted to fuck you, or everything he did was to get in your pants just the once." She couldn't have it both ways, and she'd rather it be neither. She'd rather believe Colin wanted her and that he'd be back for more.

Brad knew Colin better than she did, and if Brad said the man was freaked out by the lines they'd crossed, she'd have to accept it. Besides, Colin was slowly coming round. He'd called Brad yesterday, even if he sounded pissed on the phone when Becca picked up. Becca told him Brad was working late. She hoped Colin went by, and the two hashed things out. That would also explain why Brad spent the night at the office.

Unless something happened.

Ms. Thing dug her nails into Becca's pants, retracted them, then hooked them in again. Becca had been motionless longer than the cat was willing to wait for breakfast.

"Yeah, yeah. I'll feed you."

But first she'd open the drapes and let some light into the bedroom. She pulled on the heavy purple fabric, and the sun poured inside as if it had been waiting right outside her window.

She winced against the brightness. She needed coffee. She needed Brad.

Maybe Lorena presented him with the same offer she'd extended Becca.

No. Becca would expect any other guy she'd dated to jump at such an opportunity, but Brad wasn't any other guy. If his mother had him choose between the company and his relationship with Becca, he'd at least talk to Becca about it.

Becca groaned. She was thinking herself into a frenzy. Coffee. She needed coffee, for her morning to get back on track. Brad would probably be in a meeting about the company's future by now. He'd call her when he was free, and they'd have the afternoon to catch up. And make out.

She grabbed her cell phone on the way to the kitchen, and called her favorite nail parlor.

"This is Becca Keith. Can I swing by for a quick mani at around eleven?"

Appointment booked, she started up the cappuccino machine, and opened the refrigerator door to scrounge for breakfast. The turkey ham Brad had brought over was the only protein other than three possibly expired eggs. Still, there was sandwich bread. She gasped. No mayo.

She filled Ms. Thing's bowl with cat food and switched the cappuccino maker off again. She'd have to go out for breakfast.

* * * *

It was late for breakfast but the perfect time for brunch, and its name was pizza. The greasy, meaty kind. Becca reached for the last piece and looked at her turquoise nails. Nice and summery.

Maintaining a decent manicure was no easy feat for a painter, but Becca didn't mind the time or money regular up-keeping demanded. She liked her nails done in happy colors. She liked watching them draw stripes in the air, while she painted a wall with her brush.

She didn't put on makeup most days, and barely ever spent more time on her hair than it took to pull it up in a loose bun. She liked having one thing that was completely and totally hers. Her little beauty regime.

She wiggled her fingers. Brad would probably laugh at her choice. He liked red. The darker, the better.

Where was he, anyway? It was almost noon. Was the stupid meeting still going?

She carefully pulled her phone out of her *new,* bright-yellow bag, early birthday gift for herself. She speed-dialed Brad, but it rang until it went to voicemail.

Because Becca was an idiot, who forgot his cell phone was at her place.

Try number two—his office.

"Miller Co. This is Sarah. How may I help you?"

"Hey, it's Becca. Is he with Lorena all morning?"

Pause.

Those never boded well.

"Sarah?"

"Hi, Becca. He… There's been some trouble here."

"What trouble? Is he okay? Did something happen to him?"

"Nothing happened"—Sarah dropped her voice to a whisper—"except for him and Lorena yelling at each other for half an hour, and then him rushing out with a demented smile on his face. I was sure he'd be with you."

"He was smiling? Did he kill her?"

"No. She's alive and still fuming."

"Thanks, Sarah. I'll check his place. Maybe he went home to crash."

"Probably. When you find him, tell him I'm in awe." She raised her voice to normal pitch again, and added, "I'll tell Mr. Miller you called. Have a nice day."

Becca smiled. "You too, Sarah. And don't feed the dragon lady."

Sarah laughed, and Becca wondered for the millionth time how someone so genuine had survived being Lorena's assistant before Brad replaced his mother.

Becca tried Brad's home number next, and when he didn't answer there either, checked her own voicemail. He could have called while she was on the phone with Sarah.

He hadn't.

Becca paid for her pizza and left for home. He'd probably be waiting for her, and she'd make sure he was properly rewarded for taking on his mother first thing in the morning.

* * * *

"Babe? You home?" Becca shouldered open her apartment door, slid her key out of the lock, and toed the door closed behind her.

Only Ms. Thing hurried to greet her. No surprise there. The door had been locked, and Brad never locked when he was in.

It was after one. He should have called by now. Even if he couldn't remember her number, he would have tried his own.

But she'd left his phone at home.

Relief poured through her veins in such a rush, it made her lightheaded. He *had* called, but she wasn't there to answer. Until this very moment, she hadn't realized how worried she was about him. Anything could have happened, and he wouldn't have a way to contact her. He might have been mugged or hit by a car.

She reached her bedside table, and checked his phone. Three incoming calls. One from her cell, and two from the office.

Nothing else.

Shit.

Worry swarmed over her again. Vivid mental images of him lying on the side of the road, broken and bleeding. Stabbed in his car. Having a stroke.

What? Mid-thirties were a dangerous thing.

She smacked her lips and rolled her eyes. Colin. He was with Colin. They hadn't managed to talk last night, and they were doing so now. Brad could have called, but he was probably too strung out from this morning.

She could wait a little longer.

Or not.

She was in the Recent Calls menu anyway. She tapped Colin's name, and selected *Call*. Ms. Thing jumped on her lap, and Becca ran her fingers through the cat's fur while she the phone rang.

"Didn't think I'd hear from you again, after last night." Colin sounded guarded.

Uh oh. "He fought with you too?" Brad was running high on testosterone this week.

Colin muttered something that sounded like 'fuck.' "Hey, Becca. I'm sorry, I thought he had his phone back. Yeah, it was nothing. I'm sorry."

Two apologies in a couple of seconds? Colin sounded way too contrite just for mistaking her for Brad. "Doesn't sound like nothing, if you thought he wouldn't call you again. Did you talk" — she tried to find the most innocuous way to phrase her question—"about last Friday?"

He inhaled sharply. She knew that sound. Her dad made it when he sucked on a cigarette.

"I didn't know you smoked," she said.

"I don't. It's… nothing." Just like the fight. "Listen, Becca. About Friday—"

She really, *really*, didn't want to hear whatever came next. "Never mind that. I'm sure you and Brad will figure it out." For now, she had to find her boyfriend. "What time did you speak to him? How was he?"

Colin's chuckle sounded fake. "He was fine. Had a lot of work to do."

"He apparently stayed at the office until this morning, and then told Lorena off and stormed out. Haven't heard of him since yesterday evening. I'm worried."

"That he may be cheating on you?"

Becca frowned. She grasped a curl that had escaped her messy definition of an updo and twirled it around her finger.

"No," Becca said to Colin. "That something happened to him. Why? Should I be worried about that?" Ms. Thing play-bit her finger. Becca gave her a gentle push, and the cat jumped to the floor.

Colin's split-second-long hesitation was enough to bring old insecurities back to the surface at full force. When he finally said, "Don't be silly. The man is crazy about you," it sounded rehearsed.

"Of course you'd say that. You're his best friend." Becca forced a laugh.

Colin snorted.

She'd decided to let him and Brad sort things out, but she couldn't stay silent now. "What happened between you two? Why did you fight? Was it because you and I... I mean if you regretted it, I'm sorry. I had fun, and I tend to like having fun, but it's possible you didn't. And I'm sorry. But you two have been friends for a while; don't turn this into a self-fulfilling prophecy. Things don't need to be awkward just 'cause you said they would. Unless Brad isn't as okay with this as he says he is."

"That's not it, Becca." He huffed. "It doesn't feel right saying this when he's not present, but you're a great lay. That didn't come out right. *Fuck*."

"I'm a great fuck?"

"No. That's not—"

"I'm not a great fuck?" She smirked, but her gut twisted. A great fuck. She always thought she had to be amazing in bed to get guys to like her, but the way Colin said it, it didn't sound as a compliment.

"I can't seem to make sense today. I'm sorry. Talk to Brad." He hung up before she could say she'd only called him because she *couldn't* talk to Brad.

Because Brad was nowhere to be found.

Chapter Eighteen

Okay, this was getting scary.

Brad hadn't answered his landline throughout the day, and Becca had eventually gone to his place to make sure he wasn't lying helpless on the floor. He wasn't there, and there were no signs he'd been by at all. She'd returned home and tried to do things other than call him again and again, but her mind kept going back to him while she watched TV or bugged Ms. Thing, who wanted to sleep.

Becca's phone rang in the evening, and her heart skipped a beat. A glance at the screen showed it was Amanda.

"Hey, you." She had to keep this short. Brad might call.

If he did, he'd have to try again. Like she'd been trying for hours.

"Hey. You busy?"

Not really. "Doing some tidying up. Everything okay?"

"Yup. I felt chatty, but I guess we can catch up when you're not doing housework. Or sleeping with that gorgeous man of yours. Whom I totally approve of."

Becca laughed. Pity she couldn't say the same about Amanda's fiancé, but to each their own. "If you wait till I'm not doing either, you'll be waiting for a while."

"Now you're just bragging."

"I'll call you tomorrow to brag in detail."

"Please do. You know I live vicariously through you." Amanda's fiancé insisted on waiting until they were married to consummate their relationship.

Becca couldn't fathom being in a sexless relationship, but Amanda insisted she was happy. The more often and loudly Amanda proclaimed her happiness, the less inclined Becca was to believe her, but she let people make their own choices. Even when all she wanted was to slap some sense into them and yell that their fiancé was as charismatic as a slab of wood and just as likely to make them happy.

Unlike Brad.

Or Colin, who was charisma personified.

God, Becca had too much on her plate, even for a girl with her healthy appetite.

She hung up with the promise to buy Amanda a drink soon, and got busy with housework she'd been putting off for days. If mind-numbing manual labor didn't get her mind off Brad, nothing would.

Of course, she'd thought the same for reality TV, and that hadn't worked.

Still, she tried. She cleaned her kitchen and scrubbed her bathroom until she could see her reflection on every single surface, *but still she thought of Brad.* Only this time, he wasn't in pain or bleeding. He was tangled in someone else's sheets. Someone else's legs.

So weird that she hadn't worried about him cheating until she spoke to Colin.

Becca hated getting attached. It went against her nature. She had a cat instead of a dog because she could trust Ms. Thing to take care of herself if Becca decided to spend the night with a hot stranger. As if summoned, Ms. Thing rubbed her entire length against Becca's calf, before using it as a scratching post. Becca let her. The demanding fluff-ball had wormed its way into her heart.

Just like Brad.

She'd always been ready to flee — her studies, her jobs, her lovers. Her life aspiration had been to grow into a crazy old cat lady with a ton of sex in her past and lots of charity work in her future. And then this sweet man, with whom she'd only meant to sleep once, pulled her into his life and made her feel safe and loved and cherished.

Brad anchored her. The unprecedented sense of security he provided made her happy at the same time it terrified her. When she'd realized she was in love with him, that she would give up all other men for him, she'd wanted to break things off and run. Move to another city to get over him, if need be.

For a while, she thought it was the sex keeping Brad interested. He hadn't had enough before he met her, and he loved how open she was to experimentation. Once the novelty wore off, he'd leave. Men tended to, which was why she always left first. Becca gave it a week, then two, then stopped counting, and still the novelty didn't wear off. Whenever she met Brad's gaze, she *felt* him love her, if that was possible. He didn't say the words; it was too soon, after all. Too soon for her to be allowing a man to consume her every waking thought.

When she'd suggested a threesome for her birthday, she'd expected it to add some distance between them, not bring them closer. She meant to show him she wasn't hardwired for exclusivity. The third person would act as a buffer to slow down emotional attachment, without the complications an open relationship would bring. Sex simplified things. It put feelings into perspective.

She remembered Colin's gaze as he drove into her. Open. Soft. Vulnerable. And before that, the night the two of them stayed up talking… The pain in his eyes, the understanding and sympathy when she talked about her father's rejection couldn't be faked. There was more to Mr. Daniels than the shallow persona he shoved in people's faces, and the glimpse he'd allowed her had her yearning for more.

"You're nothing like the women I go for, which only makes it worse."

She'd tried to brush off his words, only use them as an argument for going through with her plans for the night, but they'd stayed with her.

"If we do it and like it, we can always keep doing it." What got into her, to make her say that? She should have discussed things with Brad first. Shouldn't have gone through with it.

"I want you. *If I were looking for something different, I wouldn't be here."* She believed him, and that moment he was all she wanted. But she'd always want Brad. Shit. What was supposed to be all about desire had deepened the intimacy between Brad and her, and added an extra layer she didn't feel equipped to deal with.

Ms. Thing obviously got bored. She abandoned Becca and jumped on the armchair, where she curled into a ball and watched Becca disinterestedly for a heartbeat, before closing her eyes.

Becca shook her head and focused on wiping the glass pane of the window. The deal was for a one-time thing, on her birthday. If Colin was up for it, he and Brad would take her together. She'd never had two men enter her before, and the anticipation thrilled and intimidated her. She could imagine them stretching her, pushing inside her in tandem, their moans echoing off the walls.

Brad was mild mannered but headstrong, and Colin was a rebel with a golden heart. Golden, like his hair. Like his skin, that seemed almost pale next to Brad's tan. Her boys were an incredible combination of darkness and light, inside and out, and Becca couldn't wait to be between them.

Her boys. Odd way to think of the one of them she wasn't dating. He was to be her birthday present and nothing more, but would one more time with him be enough, when she knew he'd be the last guy she'd ever fuck other than Brad?

That was, if Brad wasn't with another woman now. If he was, all bets were off, and Becca could go back to fucking any hot guy she pleased.

Colin's wide chest came to mind, bare and smooth. Brad's rock-hard thighs that easily held her weight when he pounded her into the wall.

She didn't want another hot guy. She wanted them.

Him. Brad. Her boyfriend, with whom she was very much in love.

And maybe Colin could join them more than once, if they set clear boundaries.

She snorted. Screw boundaries. This was about flesh and blood and lust, and all the beauty their bodies could make together.

Yeah… Cleaning? So *not* working, as a distraction.

Maybe a drink would hit the spot.

In her pre-Brad days, when something ate at her, she went out and found a guy to make her forget for an hour or for the night. Perhaps she should do the same now. Not like her *boyfriend* cared that she was going out of her mind.

She looked down her t-shirt to the oversized sweat pants and her frayed flip-flops. Comfy as her attire was, it didn't exactly boost her confidence, and the longer Brad didn't get in touch, the bigger her need for validation grew.

Becca tossed the duster on the kitchen counter and came back for Ms. Thing. "It's bed time for you," she said.

The cat meowed a protest when Becca gathered her in her arms, but as soon as her paws touched the mattress of the double bed, she made herself comfortable and continued her nap.

Becca closed her bedroom's door behind her and headed toward the bathroom. Shower, makeup, something short, and a visit to the nearest bar should help her mood.

She stripped off her clothes, adjusted the temperature, and stepped under the jet. The heat and pressure of the water soothed her body and her nerves. It felt like an embrace. A caress. A warm massage.

She pulled her hair out of the way, and the water pelted the back of her neck and split in two streams that cascaded down her breasts. Her skin broke out in goosebumps, and her nipples stood erect. She grazed one tip with her open palm and shivered.

All the tension of the day was funneled into an imperative need for release. She unhooked the handshower and knelt on the cold tiles. Holding on to the faucet with one hand, she used the other to aim the jet of hot water at her clitoris. A jolt ran through her, but she couldn't come like this.

She needed something inside her. Brad's hard cock. Colin's long fingers. Both of them. One pushing inside her pussy, while the other fucked her ass. Hands pinching her flesh. Opening her wider. Brad climbing up her body and forcing his cock between her open lips. Holding her in place until she gagged, and then spurting his cum down her throat while Colin pinched her clit and bit her breast, still thrusting inside her.

Her hips bucked so hard, she almost plummeted down, face first. She adjusted her grip on the faucet, and the water turned cold, shocking her out of her fantasy.

Just as well. Thinking of Brad and Colin was good for stoking the fire, but she was no closer to release than she'd been before.

She hurriedly soaped up her body, shampooed her hair, and rinsed. She needed to be outside and inebriated as soon as possible. While at it, she could find an inconsequential someone to take the edge off and keep her occupied for a couple of fun hours. Getting some strange would help her cope with her worries and blow off steam.

Even if Brad had a valid excuse for being incommunicado all day, he'd never know.

But she would, and she'd have to live with it.

Just the drink, then.

And she'd first swing by Brad's apartment once more. Maybe he'd gone home and crashed.

She wrapped a towel around her curls and applied foundation. She'd call Amanda and see if they could meet her for drinks. If not, Becca would go out, drink, flirt, and return home alone, to worry some more until she fell asleep.

She was pulling her still-wet hair in a tight bun, when the bathroom door opened behind her. In the foggy mirror, she made out Brad's tall, broad silhouette leaning against the door frame. Tension rolled off her body in a wave, and she all but sagged against the sink.

He was all right, and he was home. Back to her.

But where had he been?

Pushing relief aside, she straightened and squared her shoulders. "You almost missed me," she said.

"I miss you every moment I'm not with you."

Cheesy, but it made warmth blossom in her belly. "You could have fooled me." She unscrewed her mascara, meaning to do her eyelashes, but her hand trembled. Afraid she'd poke her eye out, she stood there, brush hovering idly.

"I'm sorry I didn't call. I needed to figure things out." He made no move to approach her.

She was naked, and he stood ten feet away. That never happened. A sliver of bare thigh was usually enough for him to pounce on her, but now he wasn't trying to touch her. He was keeping his distance.

"Did you fuck someone else?" Her voice was calm, hiding the turmoil inside.

"No." The answer came fast enough to be true, but in the mirror he uncrossed his arms and raked his fingers through his hair. He was lying. Of all the people in her life, he was the one she'd bet would never lie. Never hurt her.

Never say never.

She let the mascara brush fall in the sink, and watched it form a black streak as it circled the drain. She wanted to throw things at him. Make him hurt the way he'd hurt her. She wanted to cry.

But she wasn't that kind of girl. She was the girl who made guys laugh and come, and then made them ask for more. She'd ride Brad one last time, remind him what he'd turned his back on, and then kick him out of her apartment and her life.

She turned to face him and raised both arms over her head, pretending to fix her hair. She knew what her bouncing breasts usually did to him. "Since you're here, I could stay in." She sashayed to him, feeling anything but the prowling predator. His gaze usually made her feel like a goddess. Now she couldn't help but feel her belly jiggle. Her thighs rub together. All this time he said he saw her, and she believed him. Now she wondered if he finally lost the rose-tinted glasses and didn't much like the real her.

Her eyes stung, and her throat burned, and her heart hurt.

When Brad didn't reach for her, she undid his belt and pulled it out of its loops. "We could fuck right here," she said.

He stayed her hand, and she finally looked into his eyes. They were bloodshot.

"We need to talk." He smelled like he'd replaced his cologne with bourbon.

The tremor in his voice lowered her defenses long enough for Becca to see he wasn't unmoved. He was hurting.

She dropped the cold, bitchy act with no conscious thought. "What happened? Did Lorena sell the company?" How could Becca have been so stupid? How could she have allowed her insecurities to cloud her reason? Brad had fought with his mother, because his mother sold the company. Because she took away his job. And Becca's. And Brad couldn't come home and talk about it, because—

"She made you choose, didn't she? Me or Miller Co. Is that why you stayed away? To make up your mind?" She'd speculated enough today. She wouldn't assume she knew his choice, even if worry gnawed at her.

Brad frowned. "What? No. God, no. I was the one to set ultimatums this time, baby. I'd never give you up. Not for the company, not for anything." He uncrossed his arms and pulled her closer, and Becca felt the anger and hurt that had kept her spine ram-rod straight sap away.

She melted into his embrace and tucked her head under his chin, inhaling deeply. Under the alcohol lay his unique scent, the one her brain translated to 'home.' It was tempting to just stay there, clinging to him, but she needed answers. "What happened this morning? What ultimatum?" she asked.

He disentangled himself from her and took hold of her hand, to lead her to the living room. "Sit. And better make yourself comfortable, because my mother is the least complicated part of the story."

Becca sank back into the sofa and folded her legs beneath her. Brad sat on the armchair across from her, and the abating sense of dread began pushing its way back into her thoughts.

"I spent the night at the office" —

Well, duh.

— "but instead of compiling the report my mother wanted, I looked into the company's finances. *Really* looked. And I found all kinds of little discrepancies that added up to several hundred thousand dollars. Guess where the trail of signatures led."

"Lorena?"

Brad nodded. "Even when my father was alive. She didn't deny it when I confronted her. Just told me to leave sleeping dogs lie."

"And what did you say?"

His smile was tired, but no less brilliant than usual. "That I'll go public with the info unless she returns the money and pulls out of the company completely. She has till Friday to decide, but she called off the meeting for the sale, so I guess she'll take that time to figure out a way to do so and make the whole thing seem like her own idea."

"That's amazing, Brad. Why didn't you tell me sooner?" And where had he been all day?

"I had to figure out some stuff. Drove around most of the morning, and spent the rest of the day on the beach."

"Not inside a bottle?"

He sniffed himself and huffed. "Last drink was hours ago, I swear."

"Were you trying to drown the memory of your fight with Lorena?" She was pretty sure that wasn't the case.

Brad shook his head. "There's something else…" He clenched his fists on the armrests. "Colin."

Right. Colin. That's what had him so upset. And she was stupid to have worried herself sick.

"I kissed him."

— *the fuck?*

Chapter Nineteen

Brad held up his finger. "Please let me say it, or I never will."

She closed her mouth and tried to process the information, but before she could, Brad went on.

"Yesterday afternoon, before I came to see you, I went to find him at the gym. I cornered him and forced him to tell me why he wouldn't return my calls or answer my texts. He said he loved" — he scrunched his face — "fucking you, and it scared him. He was afraid he'd develop feelings and get hurt."

"Feelings?" Becca tried to form a coherent sentence, but her brain wouldn't cooperate. Colin was afraid he'd develop feelings for her. The fleeting thought crossed her mind that this was all a game the two friends played at her expense, but she could never see Brad being so heartless. And Colin… "He said it would be easier if I were his type," she muttered. "That it'd just be physical attraction. I thought he was just playing his part."

"He talked about developing feelings for both of us, Becca." Brad made a visible effort to keep his voice steady. To hold her gaze. "I don't know what I was thinking, but I kissed him. Not a peck on the lips. A full-on kiss. I liked it way too much. It scared me, and it made me feel like I'd betrayed you, so I fled."

She didn't know what to say. What to think. How to feel. "Did you want to be with him when you came to me?" She was too naked for this conversation. She pulled the throw over her body and focused on straightening a tassel.

"No. Becca, look at me."

She wouldn't. She wanted to be upset about it. Anger would be good. Anything but this pain that sliced deeply and left her raw and exposed. He'd kissed a guy — that wasn't a big deal by itself. But he'd never told her he was attracted to Colin. Never even hinted at wanting something more than her. With Brad, she'd felt enough. The illusion was now shattered.

"Look at me," Brad said again.

She lifted her chin defiantly. "What? You're into Colin. What am I supposed to say?"

"I left him to come tell you what I'd done and ask you to help me figure things out, but then… All I could think of was that I wanted to kill my mother for hurting you. When I had to go to work, I didn't want to just throw this thing at you and let you deal with it alone. I decided to talk to you when I got home."

"But you didn't come home. *All day.*"

"I wasn't ready to see you. Colin came to the office last night, to ask why I'd kissed him. Why I'd run. One thing led to another, and he ended up—" He buried his face in his palms. "God. This is hard to say."

Had they fought? Kissed again? Fucked?

When Brad met her gaze again, his big brown eyes were pleading. "He knelt down in front of me and sucked my dick. And I let him. And I loved it. He fingered my ass, and I wanted more. I still want more."

No, wait. This wasn't pleading. If anything, his eyes held a challenge.

Becca opened her mouth to ask what the fuck he expected her to do about it, but no words came out. She didn't do pregnant pauses or dramatic sighs, damn it. She always cut to the chase. So why was she stalling, wondering how stupidly hot the sight of Colin blowing Brad had to be? Brad had cheated on her. Pure and simple. It didn't matter that he'd done so with a guy, instead of another woman. She didn't even care about the act itself. What counted was the deceit.

But did it count when he himself had been surprised by what happened? And when the other person was a guy she'd had sex with days earlier? Someone she hoped to—no, *planned on* having sex with again this Saturday? Did she honestly mind sharing Brad with Colin, as long as she got a piece of both of them?

She grimaced. Way to cheapen her feelings for Brad. "Do you want to be with him?" she asked.

"I don't think I'm gay, but he obviously did it for me, and... You don't want to hear this. I'm so sorry."

But she did want to hear it. She felt about a hundred-and-thirty-seven kinds of dirty for wanting more detail, rather than setting her boundaries. Unless her boundaries were just wider than those her mother hoped they'd be. "Not what I asked," she said. "Do you want to be with him more than you want to be with me?"

"No." His open gaze left no room for her to doubt his honesty. "I want him, though, Becca. And I want you. I don't know if I'm bisexual or—"

"How about you stop trying to label yourself, and just go with what you feel?"

"I'm trying to make sense of it. Until yesterday, I'd never considered touching a guy this way, but now I don't want to stop. I've been taught not to ask for things, and I'm so grateful for everything you've given me, but I need to ask you this."

"What? Absolution? I'm not your fucking priest, and you don't have to worry about me telling on you."

"That's not— Shit, Becca, I love you."

The words rattled inside her brain and made her ears buzz. "*This* is how you tell me? 'A dude blew me, and also I love you'?" She expected to sound shrill, but the words came out raspy.

He ran his fingers through his hair and sighed. "I meant to do a whole song-and-dance on Saturday. Give you your gift and tell you I love you. There'd be candle light."

"That would probably go down better." She wanted to laugh and cry at the same time. She hated how much power he had over her emotional stability. "So what do you want me to do? Give you a hall pass?" She could do that. She *would* do that. She was okay with Brad experimenting, if they set some ground rules. She'd lost the moral high ground anyway, when she fucked his best friend.

Brad leaned forward, elbows on his knees. "No. I want to try something else. A different kind of exclusive. I don't want to choose. I want you both, and not just for this Saturday."

Never in a million years would she have seen this coming, and she prided herself in being prepared for any scenario. She clenched her jaw.

He glanced at the ceiling. At his feet. At the coffee table. Anywhere but in her direction. "Because of you, I no longer care what people think. I don't know if there's a God, but if He exists, I doubt he'll keep me out of heaven because I want to be happy, and you and Colin make me happy. Both of you. Together."

"Oh." *Together.* For more than sex. Colin was supposed to slow things down, damn it, not throw her head-first into more complicated feely stuff. He'd told Brad he could fall for Becca. And Brad obviously felt something for him, or he wouldn't be suggesting this.

Could Brad love two people at a time?

Could she?

"I mean all of us in a relationship," Brad said. As if he hadn't been clear.

"Yeah. I got it," she snapped. Her turn to avert her gaze. She didn't need him reading her face while she tried to decide how she felt about things. "How do you see that working, exactly? Will it be all of us together, all the time? Do I have to take turns sleeping with each of you? Will you book Tuesdays and Thursdays for me, and Mondays and Wednesdays for Colin?" She didn't sound half as irritated as she meant to. More like she wanted actual answers. Did she? Was she considering this?

"There wouldn't be any rules. Well, except for the fact that none of us would be sleeping around. I don't have all the answers."

Now she glared at him. "Ya think?"

"We can figure things out as we go. If you and Colin want to try this, we can all start dating. At the same time. Go to a movie" — would she get to blow them both? — "and *actually* watch it."

"So you see dinners for three in romantic restaurants in our future? This will be interesting. *Could* be interesting, I mean. Hypothetically."

"Becca, I spent all day trying to work things through in my head. Nobody is going to like this. Well, except for us. We'll have a hell of a time." His laugh sounded forced. "Everyone's going to judge us, but I decided I don't give a shit. I've already more or less cut all ties with my mother, and if my friends don't like my choices, I can't really be bothered with them."

She couldn't hold back a smile. "I see I've rubbed off on you."

"More than that. You've opened my eyes, Becca. Made me see what it's like to live for yourself, and I want to do that. I want to go after what makes me happy. Stop wearing ties to work. Maybe take a cooking class." He grinned. "And I want to be able to be with the people I want to be. I love you — cat's out of the bag now — and you're the only one who can influence my choices. I want us in this together. If you say no, what happened with Colin will be the end of it. But if you say yes, Saturday can be the beginning.

"We can all spend time together. Enjoy each other's company without holding back. Ask for what we want. Kiss. Make love. Fuck. Play video games and watch Battlestar Galactica." He paused and tilted his head, his gaze soft. "Fall in love, maybe?"

She realized she hadn't said the words back when he told her how he felt. Better that way, if she decided to cut her losses. It would hurt both of them less.

He splayed his hands on his legs, palms facing upward. "I've made my case, but we'll do whatever you want."

And what the hell would that be?

Becca had two choices. She could freak out and play possessive, which didn't come natural and wasn't fair anyway, since she'd slept with Colin—and with Brad's blessing—or she could see this for the opportunity it was. She'd never meant to be with just one man, but she would make that sacrifice for Brad.

Only now Brad said she didn't have to. She could have both him and Colin. Be free with both of them.

Her main hang-up was that Brad wouldn't be able to handle what he suggested, but she'd thought the same about him watching her with Colin, and was proven completely wrong. Brad had thought this through. They could make it work.

"At least you're not running for the hills." He barked the fakest laugh she'd ever heard.

"That's 'cause I live here. Also, I'm kind of into you." Understatement of the year. She was in love with him, and could love Colin too, if she let herself. The idea exhilarated her and sent jolts of lust to the apex of her thighs, but she'd been raised to think relationships were only meant for couples.

Screw that. She'd also been taught love should only be between a man and a woman, and that sex was dirty and wrong, but she'd seen these theories for the bullshit they really were — though sex could be *incredible* when it was dirty and wrong.

What Brad proposed would allow her to openly express her desire for another man and act on it, without betraying her boyfriend. It would let Brad be the person he wanted to be. The man Lorena Miller had repeatedly tried to smother.

It would make them both happy.

Becca smiled. He was right. Nobody would approve, but she wasn't seeking anyone's approval. "Do you think you can get Colin on board? He disappeared after we had sex. He won't be easy to find now that he's sucked off his BFF." She felt the crazy glint in her eyes, but there was no toning it down. Even if Colin didn't go through with this, she and Brad would never get back to where they were before Friday. It was scary but not necessarily bad. Not if they moved forward.

"You mean you're up for it? I don't want to pressure you into anything." Brad looked incredibly cute, trying to keep the glee from his voice.

Becca nodded.

"The three of us can be so good together," he said, "but you're my girlfriend, and if you're not entirely comfortable..."

"You're overselling it." Becca bit her lip and tossed back the throw. She spread her legs, and raked her nails

161

up her thighs, loving how he followed her every move with his gaze. She hadn't lost him. Not even close. And if Colin played along, she'd have more than she ever imagined. "I guess I could be persuaded," she said.

Brad was next to her before the words left her lips. He closed his large palms over her hips, shifted her body, and pulled so she lay beneath him on the couch. "I'm prepared to do all the grunt work," he whispered, leaning down to place open-mouthed kisses along her neck.

She giggled. His five-o'clock shadow tickled, but it wasn't the reason for her giddiness. Her heart soared, and her body ached for his touch. Nothing felt as right as having him inside her.

Becca reached for the lapel of his wrinkled shirt, but Brad grasped her wrist and pushed it down on the couch. "Let me," he said. "I owe you."

Technically, he owed Colin, but as his lips and tongue mapped her breasts, Becca decided not to correct him. Brad grazed the underside of one breast with his nose, raising goose bumps, and then closed his lips around the nipple. He squeezed the other breast just to this side of pain, while he sucked and nibbled.

The different stimuli confused Becca. She wanted to give into everything at the same time. She dug her fingers into his hair. Thick and longer than Colin's, it offered a perfect lever for her to drive his head lower. Much as her tits appreciated the attention, her cunt needed it more.

She pressed him to her, wanting him to devour her, wanting to lose herself into him.

Brad obliged. He kissed a path down her stomach, caressing her side down to her hip. She was ticklish above her hipbone, and she giggled, but the giggle was cut short when he grazed her inner thigh with his teeth.

She moaned, and he bit a little harder. Worried the tender flesh with his teeth and lips. There'd be a mark there in the morning, and Becca couldn't care less.

Brad moved his hand to the apex of her thighs, and ran his thumb along her bare slit. Becca lifted her hips, eager for more of his touch. His laugh was muffled by her thigh.

"Not funny." But she smiled. She loved him teasing her, as long as he followed it up with one of those nerve-tingling full-body orgasms.

Brad gave her thigh a last, butterfly-light kiss, and then did with his tongue what he'd done with his finger. And again, this time brushing her clitoris on the upstroke. Becca whimpered and tightened her grip on his hair. He finally pushed his tongue inside her, and Becca ground against his mouth with a sigh. That drove her crazy but wasn't enough to make her come. Not even when he pressed his thumb on her clitoris and rubbed like he did now.

Almost there, but not. "Thought you said you owed me," she managed through gritted teeth, pumping up her hips to meet the thrusts of his tongue.

He lifted his head to look at her. "You're right. And I pay my debts." Still circling her clit, he twisted his wrist and plunged two fingers inside her.

She jerked her hips in surprise but dropped her head back and gave in to the sensation of his long, talented fingers driving in and out of her pussy. She'd rather have his weight pressing down on her, the smell of his aftershave filling her nostrils, and his hard cock pulsating inside her, but this was a close second. The friction drove her pleasure up a notch with each thrust. A ball of white-hot fire swirled in her center, nudging her closer to the edge. When he closed his lips over her clit and sucked, letting his lower teeth graze the sensitive button, she was done for.

She barely bit back three little yet so-fucking-powerful words, as her body convulsed with the release of the tension he'd built up in her.

She clamped her thighs around his head and held him in place as she rode out her orgasm, loving his moans. He moaned with the satisfaction of pleasuring her. No greater turn-on than a guy who loved making her come more than he cared about his own dick.

Still not fully in control of her limbs, Becca pulled him up by the hair for a kiss that had him panting too. "I want you inside me," she said.

"Not tonight. I haven't slept in more than thirty-six hours." He rolled to the side, taking her with him, and pulled as much of the throw over them as he could.

Becca was glad for the wide couch. She'd hate to have to move when he'd jellified her legs. She kissed him again, tasting herself on her lips, then turned her back to him and scooted closer to fit the curve of his body. His arm was under her head, and she knew her neck would be stiff in the morning, but she wouldn't trade the sense of safety and rightness for a more comfortable sleeping arrangement.

"I have to call Colin in the morning," Brad whispered in her hair, "if he'll still talk to me."

"You think he regrets what he did?" she asked, her eyes drifting shut.

"I think I acted like an ass afterward. I froze. Didn't know how to deal, and I felt bad about us. You-and-me us. It may have seemed like I brushed him off."

"And then you didn't call." Becca chewed on the inside of her cheek.

"And then I didn't call." He tugged on one of her curls. He did that when they talked about things that made him uncomfortable. "I wanted to talk with you first, so I'd know what to say to him."

"You think once you're done groveling, he'll be open to the idea?"

She felt him shrug behind her. "I hope so. If he gets over his fear of being a normal human with feelings, he'll have nothing else holding him back. He's never cared about what others think, and he has a solid support system." There might be a hint of bitterness or jealousy in Brad's voice. "His parents are the best, most understanding people on the planet, and his asshole brother has written him off anyway."

"His brother?" She knew someone had hurt Colin— figured out as much that night she and Brad stayed at his place.

"Yeah, Alan is his older brother, and a complete prick. In his narrow little worldview, Colin's somehow to blame for everything that's gone wrong with Alan's life, including Alan being stuck in a town he hates. Last time they met, Alan blamed Colin for their father falling off the roof and breaking his leg. And then he called him a fucking faggot."

"Sounds like a charmer."

"If I ever meet him up close, I'm punching his lights out."

Becca smiled. This was her lover. The man she loved, who would do anything to protect and defend those he cared about. "He's lucky to have you," she said.

"In the morning we'll see if he feels the same."

"I'm sure he does. If not, I'll give it a try too. I have an idea about how to bring him over to the dark side," she said.

"Offer him cookies?" His cock was half hard against her ass, and Becca couldn't resist a little wiggle.

Brad groaned, and she laughed. "Kind of. Let's see how things go with the two of you first. Assuming you still feel the same way about this in the morning, when you don't smell like a brewery."

"I'm not drunk. Just exhausted—physically and mentally."

Becca nodded. "Goodnight."

Brad pulled her closer and laid a kiss on her shoulder. She felt his chest rise and fall with each breath, and could tell when he drifted off. Despite her own fatigue, Becca couldn't sleep; she was too busy thinking of all the delicious things coming her way.

Chapter Twenty

As she'd predicted, she woke up with a crick on her neck, but the hard cock digging into her lower back more than made up for it. Sometime during the night, he'd lost his clothes. She pumped her hips, and Brad mirrored her movement. He glided his free hand down her stomach and between her legs, and she spread them to accommodate him.

He was the first man who hadn't made her feel she had to suck in her belly when she was naked with him.

He slid his fingers between her folds and rubbed her clit, but Becca was too impatient to enjoy the foreplay. She lifted her leg and draped it over his as he spooned her. Brad didn't need a written invitation to enter her. They both loved this kind of wakeup, and indulged in it whenever their morning schedule allowed for it.

"What time is it?" Brad asked, moving in and out of her.

Becca reached over to the coffee table for his cell phone and lit the screen. "It's eight. Shouldn't you be getting ready for work?" Not that she wanted him to stop what he was doing. *Ever.*

"I'm taking the day off." He swiveled his hips and pumped, and she dropped the phone.

＊＊＊＊

Give it a few days, man. I'll get over it.

Brad showed Becca the text and shrugged. "He sent this after my call went to voicemail. He doesn't want to talk to me."

She saw his effort to seem cool. "He'll get over it. He said so himself."

"Think you can make that happen sooner rather than later?" He held his phone out to her.

Becca reached for it and nodded. "I can definitely try."

He climbed over her, hopped off the couch, and stretched, allowing her a perfect view of his sculpted back, ass, and thighs. Who'd have known she'd end up with a guy this hot? Two guys this hot, if Colin agreed to what she'd suggest. Her mom would freak out if she met either of them. She always told Becca no good-looking man would be interested in her unless she lost weight and dressed more appropriately.

Appropriate. That was an adjective Becca never managed to squeeze herself into. To be honest, she'd stopped trying a long time ago.

"You call him, and I'll go get breakfast," Brad said, pulling on his pants. "I'll run by my place and get some clothes too. Taking you out to dinner tonight." As if great morning sex and a lie-in weren't enough. It could be lingering guilt over his sexy times with Colin, but Becca wouldn't look a gift horse in the mouth. Breakfast in bed—or in a generally prone position—was in her top five pastimes. "Will you let Ms. Thing out of the bedroom and feed her, please?" She could be greedy at times, but he didn't seem to mind that.

"Yes, Ma'am." Brad saluted and ducked down for a long, lingering kiss, before he went to tend to the cat.

Becca smiled and called up Colin's number on Brad's cell. She carefully dialed the digits on her own phone and pressed *Call*.

"Colin Daniels." Colin sounded overly cheerful. He was in salesman mode.

"Hey, sexy."

"Becca. Good morning. Brad still missing?" His tone changed to something between guarded and worried.

"Oh, no. He's here, and he's fine."

"Thanks for letting me know, but a client just walked in, so we'll talk later."

She bit back a laugh at the obvious lie. "Nobody walked in, Colin. You just want to hang up because you blew my boyfriend and you're too embarrassed to talk to me. It's okay. We're over it."

Silence.

Had someone actually shown up?

"What do you want?" he asked. "To scare me off? I'm off, Becca. It won't happen again. Brad made it clear he wasn't interested, and I'm not desperate enough to—"

"Oh, cut it out."

"Sorry?"

"You should be sorry, but then so should I, most of the time."

"Becca, I have no time for this. I fucked up, but it's over. I'm sorry I hit on Brad. I don't know what I was thinking."

"Colin, can you please shut up? I called to ask you to lunch."

"Lunch?" He chuckled. "Are you going to poison me?"

This time she did laugh. "Yeah, 'cause that's the kind of woman I am. Jealous, sneaky, and lethal."

"I can believe the last part." How could he make *that* sound suggestive?

Not the point. So not the point.

"Lunch?" she asked.

"I'm really busy."

"I'll come by your office. One o'clock." She hung up before he could put up an argument. If he wasn't in when she went to see him, she'd wait him out. She'd chase him down. Nothing would take this opportunity away from her.

Brad gave her a questioning look from the bedroom doorway, and she held both thumbs up.

"Well?" he asked.

"Well, I decided I'll just have one bagel, because I have a lunch date."

He grinned and shook his head.

Ms. Thing jumped on the couch, licking her lips, and Becca scratched the feline's neck. She'd enjoy seeing Colin squirm almost as much as she'd love convincing him to see things her way.

* * * *

Becca was ten minutes late, partly due to traffic and partly to make Colin sweat a little.

"Ms. Keith is here to see you, Mr. Daniels." Colin's assistant let her into Colin's office.

"Thank you, Simon. You can take your break now."

With the door closed behind Simon, Colin gestured for Becca to sit.

"Aren't we going out for lunch?" she asked.

"I thought we might want to keep this conversation indoors," he replied.

If she hadn't learned to look behind the mask, she wouldn't have noticed his discomfort. Colin was stretched out in his desk chair. He looked calm and collected, but she noticed how he clicked the pen over and over with his thumb. He was afraid she'd make a scene. If she wasn't set on convincing him to give Brad's idea a try, she'd let him stew a bit longer.

"Whatever you think I'm here for, you're wrong," she said.

"You've already ruled out killing me and warning me to back off your boyfriend, so I've run out of theories." He placed his pen by the notepad on his large desk and steepled his fingers on his chest.

"Brad and I want you to come to my birthday on Saturday." She should have worn something sexier than jeans and a fitted shirt, but she wanted her words, not her boobs, to get her point across.

Colin widened his eyes and worked his jaw like he'd tasted something sour.

Becca had expected a different reaction. Perhaps an eruption or a nervous chuckle. "It'll be just us, same place we met on Friday. Brad will take care of the food and the music," she said. "All you have to do is show up."

"And fuck you," he whispered. "Show up and fuck you, at the same time your boyfriend—*my best friend*—is fucking you."

"Yes." Her voice wavered, but when she spoke again, she had it under control. "Things have happened, but nothing's changed. We still want you. Both of us."

Colin rubbed his chin and arched an eyebrow. "So in this new scenario, Brad fucks me too?"

Becca could tell he was getting at something she wouldn't like, but she shrugged. "If that's what you both want."

"And you'll be okay with it." He tapped his thumbs together repeatedly. She wanted to get up and slam her palm down on them to keep them still.

"We talked about it. He told me what you did and how he enjoyed it. I think people should do the things they enjoy." Becca didn't want to share Brad's suggestion before she knew Colin was interested. She'd build up to it as she gauged his reactions. Despite her gut feeling and Brad assurances, Colin might consider what they did a one-time thing and not want to repeat it.

He stood so fast, he sent his chair rolling into the wall. "Well, I didn't enjoy fucking you, Becca, so I won't be doing that again."

The insecure girl inside, the one who always sought approval, cried out in pain. She'd been rejected before, more than once, but never for her sexual prowess. That was the one thing she knew she was good at. Her means of connecting with men.

She swallowed down the bile that bubbled up her throat, and focused on what he tried to hide from her. He'd felt the connection between them. He'd wanted her despite himself. Becca wouldn't allow him to erase that.

She gazed at him. "You *loved* fucking me. You hated that you loved it, but you loved it anyway. If Brad wasn't there, you'd have spent the whole night between my legs."

"Someone thinks highly of herself."

The irony in that sentence coming from him, of all people, was almost enough to make her burst into giggles, but she was determined not to be distracted from her goal. "I saw you, when you sank inside me. I saw how you looked at me."

"I couldn't believe I was screwing my best friend's girlfriend. Doesn't mean I wanted you. Read my lips—I don't want you." He was all but yelling, his composure gone.

She couldn't help entertaining the possibility he was telling the truth. He seemed set on convincing her; that was for certain. But his face wasn't contorted in anger. His expression was filled with pain.

She stood and studied him, taking in the vein that popped on his forehead, the long lashes shading the narrowed dark-blue eyes, the sensual lips she longed to kiss even as she wanted to slap some sense into him.

Narrowing her own eyes, she planted her hands on her hips. "Oh my God! Colin Daniels, you're Lassie-ing me."

He gave her a confused look.

"You're doing to me what that kid did to Lassie. Trying to drive me away for my own good. You don't get to make my choices for me."

"No. This isn't… I just want to be left alone."

She rounded the desk and approached him as she would a wounded animal. He jerked when she touched his arm, but she didn't retract her hand. "You're protecting yourself. Brad told me you aren't as casual about this as you pretend to be. Not about either of us."

"Brad bought the same crap I've been feeding one-night stands since I figured out what my cock was for." Despite the crass words, his reply lacked bite.

"You don't lie to women to get them to bed. You don't sell them empty promises. You show your cards, like you showed them to me." She caressed up and down his arm, his bicep taut under the silk shirt.

Colin sat rigid as a statue, not even turning to face her. "I showed you nothing. You don't know me."

"I know more than you want me to."

"The hell you do." But he didn't move when she came to stand in front of him, her breasts touching his chest.

"I know you love Brad and that you want him."

Colin shook his head but didn't speak.

"I know you want me more than you'll let yourself admit."

He narrowed his eyes, and Becca felt something hard against her thigh. If only she didn't worry jumping him on the spot would drive him away…

"I know you won't stop me if I do this." She slanted her mouth over his before he had time to speak. He put no resistance. Instead, he stepped forward, trapping her between his body and the desk. The sharp edge of the desk dug into her ass, as he brought his arms up to pin her to him and devoured her mouth. He sucked her lower lip between his and nibbled on it, before his tongue found hers.

If she wasn't careful, she'd lose control. They'd screw again, and Colin would add that to the layers of self-loathing he hid behind.

She broke the kiss and nuzzled his neck. Then she pushed at his chest with both hands until he let go and took a step back. "Come to us this Saturday," she said. "Brad thought of something new you might like."

He arched an eyebrow and licked his lips. "Something new?"

"Yup." And now was time for the final blow. "Unless you've dated a couple before."

Colin gaped at her.

"That's what I thought." She tapped his cheek lightly, turned, and walked to the exit.

He was faster than her and blocked her way. "What is it with the two of you throwing me curveballs and running away? You can't just say shit like that and make me—"

"Make you what? Hope for more? Feel free to. You won't be disappointed."

She tried to wedge past him, and he stepped away from the door, holding up his palms.

"You owe me lunch, but I'll settle for you joining us for dinner on Saturday," she said, before she hurried downstairs, where Brad was waiting to follow her and Colin to lunch, so he could show up and support her case when the time was right.

"He stood you up?" he asked, setting the car into gear. Disappointment drew his brows together and darkened his eyes.

"Nope. We talked. I was aloof and mysterious, and I think my timing was perfect. He's intrigued, if nothing else." Becca squeezed his thigh and put on her seatbelt. "Now let's get some food into me. I'm not supposed to be horny and hungry at the same time, or human lives are at risk."

Brad shook his head, a wide smile lighting up his face. "There's a burger joint round the corner. And afterward, I'll do something about your other little issue."

Colin

Chapter Twenty-One

Colin swirled the amber liquid in the tumbler. Today wasn't a beer day. It was a single-malt day. A fucking long day, possibly the first of many.

Because he wouldn't get over Becca or Brad anytime soon.

He'd thought he could. He fucked one and blew the other. He crossed the line, tasted the forbidden fruit, and was now free to get them out of his system.

When Brad didn't chase after him on Monday or call all day yesterday, Colin thought he was done. Then Brad called this morning, and Becca knew about the blow job, and they still wanted him.

Fuck.

Why couldn't they have left him alone?

Seeing Becca had hammered in how much he ached for her, and her parting words had him going crazy all day. She couldn't mean it. Dating a couple? As what? The third wheel?

He took a sip and savored the burn down his throat. Then he remembered swallowing Brad's cum, and polished off the rest of his drink in one long gulp. He needed to erase the memory.

He *was* done. Brad and Becca made him feel, and feelings led to pain. Even if Becca meant her suggestion the way she phrased it, and Brad saw things the same way, they'd at some point realize either that they didn't need him or that they could no longer be together. This little experiment was doomed to fail, and he wouldn't be one of the people torn to pieces by it.

He grabbed his phone and punched in Brad's number. If he was fast enough, he wouldn't have time to regret it.

"Hey." Brad's voice was low and thick. Bedroom voice. Was he in bed with Becca? Were they naked?

Colin rubbed his face. "You busy?"

"Not really. I'm out for food."

Colin's stomach growled, and the halo of a migraine began forming behind his eyelids. "Becca came to see me."

"I know."

"You know what she said?"

"I do." Brad sounded cautious.

"And you're on board with that?" It shouldn't matter. Colin shouldn't care. He should be the one saying no.

There was a long pause, and then Brad said, "I'm coming over."

"Don't." If he and Becca were of one mind on the subject, Brad would say so. Which meant he wasn't. Colin ought to be happy. This got him off the hook.

"We need to talk," Brad said.

Colin was tired and just wanted to rub one off and go to sleep. And not talk about what happened last night or how it wouldn't be happening again. He didn't want to hear how Brad was indulging his girlfriend's wishes but didn't care about a three-way relationship—and could Colin please turn Becca down, because Brad didn't want to disappoint her? "I'm about to go to bed. Just wanted to clear things up. Now they're clear. Goodnight."

"I'll be there in twenty."

* * * *

The sound of his doorbell made Colin jump. He'd dozed off on the couch. His stomach clenched. Had to be the alcohol, not dread over seeing Brad. That, and he should have eaten something.

"Coming," he yelled.

"Thought that was my line," Brad called from the other side of the door.

Fuck. Fuck. Double fuck.

Colin considered not getting the door, but he wasn't a pussy. He'd face Brad, let him say his peace, and then wrap things up.

He opened the door with as disinterested an expression as he could muster. Good thing too, because Brad looked better than usual, with his five-o'-clock shadow and tight T-shirt.

"Neither of you knows what *don't come over* means, huh?" Colin asked. He stepped aside for Brad to enter, and then closed the door and leaned against it. "Who buzzed you in?"

"The old lady from down the hall was coming out of the building—the one with the tiny white dog? I told her I'm staying over and you forgot to give me a copy of your downstairs keys. She's seen me around enough times to buy it."

"She probably thinks we're fucking." Colin regretted the words the moment they were out of his mouth.

"Yeah." Brad smiled. It reached his eyes, and something inside Colin eased the tiniest bit.

"So you told Becca."

"I did. May I?" Brad pointed to the couch.

"It's late."

Brad nodded. "I get it. We probably won't do much talking if I sit, anyway."

Colin was running low on humor today. He arched an eyebrow, exhaustion turning into irritation. He knew Brad's visit wouldn't be conducive to sleep.

"Not funny. I'm sorry," Brad said.

"Just for that?"

"For everything. For pressuring you to sleep with Becca, when you said no."

Here was the regret Colin had warned them about. Brad wasn't cool with him fucking his girlfriend. He probably resented them both for it, *as Colin said he would.*

Well, boo-fucking-hoo. Colin resented this Scottish-shower routine Brad put him through. "I did say no," he said. "Repeatedly. Which was more than you did at your office." Would he stop bringing up *the thing?*

"I know. I should have—"

But Colin wouldn't stop. "It's okay. I enjoyed fucking her. It was fun. Becca's body yielding, as yours hardened. You enjoyed it too. We've already had this discussion. And then you kissed me. Remember?"

Brad would deny it, of course. He'd come up with a convenient excuse about what happened on Monday, or act like nothing did. He'd probably stick with Becca another month, and then find an excuse to break up with her. He'd pretend to be Colin's friend for a while, and then gradually distance himself.

Because Brad didn't do confrontation. Going to the gym, to find Colin, had been a rare exception, and even then he'd run away.

"I didn't just enjoy it," Brad said. "I loved it. Like I loved you sucking my dick."

Colin didn't see that coming, but he hid his surprise. "Enough to tell your girlfriend, apparently. I'm honored. Does she need any pointers?" He was being nasty, but it hurt being this close to Brad and unable to joke around with him. Or touch him like he ached to. One time wasn't enough, but more could be a disaster.

Brad shoved both hands in his pockets and ducked his head. He looked like a little boy, but the glance he threw Colin was that of a man who wouldn't give up till he got what he was after. "I should have stopped you on Monday. I wanted to."

Colin chewed on his lip to keep from calling him a lying asshole.

"It felt wrong to do something without discussing it with Becca. We're supposed to be exclusive" — Brad shrugged — "unless we're both with you. She had to know. To be okay with it. But you took me in your mouth, and it was fucking incredible."

"Maybe we should sit down after all." Because Colin's legs felt as sturdy as spaghetti, unlike his rock-hard cock.

They sat across from each other, the table acting as a barrier between them, and Brad went on. "You need to understand. I've never been into guys, but I'm into you. And now Becca is okay with it, I thought…"

Colin gulped. Not enough alcohol in his system for this. "You thought what?"

"Listen, I reacted badly. I know. You opened a new world for me, and I was shocked and hated cheating on Becca, and I just had to do things in the right order. I came clean with her, and now I'm coming clean with you. I want you. I'm scared and it'll take some easing into things — figuratively and literally — but I'd like to return the favor at some point."

What should Colin say to that? Because the first answer that popped to mind was *yes, please*, but it couldn't be the correct one. Right?

Tired. Sleepy. Hungry. Moody. *Hard.*

All because of Brad.

He wouldn't let him off that easy. "Spell it out for me."

Brad licked his lips and steepled his fingers. He stared at his shoes for so long, Colin thought he changed his mind. When Brad looked up again, a devilish smirk crooked the corners of his lips. "Colin, Becca and I want to date you. We want you to join us for her birthday soiree. And I'd like the opportunity to suck your cock. Just not now, because Becca is waiting."

Migraine forgotten, Colin felt laughter bubble up in his chest. It was a new sensation, being happy. "Lorena would wash your mouth with soap for this."

"I've run out of fucks to give."

Good answer.

Brad

Chapter Twenty-Two

Brad returned to Becca's with a spring to his step and a smile on his lips. If he was ever to be struck by lightning, now was the time. He couldn't imagine his life getting any better.

He had to lie to her again, but this time he felt no guilt over it.

As soon as he crossed the threshold, she snatched the paper bags he carried and planted a smacking kiss on his lips. "I *thought* I smelled curry. The whole building is going to hate you for this, but you're my hero."

"I scratch your back. You scratch mine." He squeezed her ass and followed her to the living room, where she sat gingerly on the floor.

"Later tonight, though Indian may not be the best aphrodisiac." She tore into the naan while they both unpacked boxes. "Was the place crammed?"

"Sorry?"

She pointed to the pink elephant on the side of a carton box. "The restaurant. It's three blocks from here, and it took you forever. Was it packed?"

"Yeah. Sorry to keep you waiting." Only not really sorry, because the kiss goodnight Colin gave him still burned his lips. "Want some soda?"

184

"Yes, please." She let out an appreciative moan. "Their butter chicken is to die for."

He'd die for more of her moans. Her sighs. Colin's grunts.

Maybe he should ask to be in the middle for his birthday. He poured two glasses of soda and returned to the living room. He folded his body next to hers, and watched her enjoy her dinner. His chicken tikka smelled amazing, but didn't make his mouth water like thoughts of what was to come. He itched to share with Becca what had really kept him, but it wasn't time yet. He wouldn't want to ruin the surprise.

"Did you hear from Colin?" she asked between bites.

"No. He didn't call you either?"

She shook her head. "Nothing. I guess we have to find a backup for my birthday."

The blood drained from his head. A backup? Saturday was supposed to be about bringing in Colin, not screwing a random guy. "I thought—"

"Gotcha." She grinned. "Admit it; you were worried I meant it."

"I never know what's in that devious mind of yours." He kissed her and tasted the spices and coconut milk mingled with her distinct flavor. Going from kissing Colin to kissing Becca. He could live with that.

"Uh-oh. Someone had a naughty thought. Don't lie; I see it in your eyes." She squeezed his thigh and nodded toward the food. "Wanna leave this for later?"

Hell, yeah.

Becca

Chapter Twenty-Three

The rest of the week dragged its ass.

Brad didn't go to work on Thursday either, and Becca more than enjoyed her time with him, but she found it impossible to not think of Colin. Had he made up his mind?

Couldn't the jackass call and tell them he was game, already?

As predicted, Lorena called Brad on Thursday evening, to tell him she'd decided she needed to take care of herself and planned on a month-long holiday. As if their fight had never happened and distancing herself form Miller Co. was her own idea. She didn't give him more information, and he didn't ask, but he told Becca he'd give Lorena that month to come up with the money she'd embezzled and find a way to return it to the company.

Then they had more mind-blowing sex, and by the time Becca dozed off naked in his arms, Colin was only a distant thought in the back of her mind.

On Friday, Brad had to go by the office, and Becca found herself staring at her cell phone. Should she call Colin? Text him?

Nah. Too desperate. Not like she'd suffer a great loss if he wasn't interested. She was perfectly happy with Brad. Content.

Have you decided yet, or are you flipping a coin? she typed, and then deleted it. Snark was her go-to approach, and Colin would probably respond to it, but she'd have to try something softer if she wanted to lower his shields.

I always thought Starbuck should keep both Adama Jr. and Anders.

Nah. Too geeky and not exactly direct. Honesty was key, for him to believe they didn't just want him for a night.

I hope you come.

The four little words and their double entendre would have to do. She pressed *Send* and got the delivery report almost immediately.

Ms. Thing's demanding meows made Becca stop looking at the darkened screen. Keep busy. Feed the cat. Change the kitty litter. Pay bills. Decide what to wear on Saturday. She wanted to go with the black wrap dress with the plunging neckline and thigh-high slit. And her birthday would be the perfect excuse to break out those bejeweled stiletto-heeled sandals she'd bought on a whim and never worn.

She imagined Brad's brown eyes going almost black with desire when she undressed and stood before him in nothing but those shoes. Would Colin's gaze also feel like a lover's caress?

And she was back on Colin.

She remembered her father calling her a slut when he caught her talking with the neighbor's oldest son. She'd run into the boy—Joe or Joey or something like that—on her way back from the lake. She had on her shorts, but no shirt over her bikini top, and Joe or Joey had asked her how the water was. She was fifteen and flirty, and she enjoyed the seventeen-year-old's attention, but he hadn't as much as touched her hand when her father thundered out of the house, yelling for her to come inside.

"And put some clothes on. I don't want the entire neighborhood seeing I've raised a little slut." The disgust on her father's face had cut deeper than his words. Becca hadn't gone for a swim again that summer.

She knew better now. Knew she wasn't a slut. That her father was an overbearing miserable prude of a man. They'd found their balance and managed to be civil when they pretended to be a happy family for the same neighborhood's sake. The young girl inside her, whose self-esteem her father had systematically torn apart, now chuckled at the memory of riding Joe or Joey in her father's back yard a few years later.

What would her darling father think if he found out how she planned on celebrating her thirtieth birthday? He'd probably have a stroke.

She checked her phone. No reply from Colin. No call from Brad.

Nothing to do.

She could go to the dojo. She hadn't set foot in the martial-arts class since she'd met Brad, and she could use the outlet provided by kicking and punching a defenseless bag.

But Amanda wouldn't be teaching a class anyway. She was moving to a new place and getting ready for her wedding to Mason—*yuck*. She might be free to meet, but Becca didn't feel like pretending to be excited about floral arrangements and color patterns. If that made her a horrible friend, she'd have to make up for it by offering a shoulder for Amanda to cry on after her marriage crashed and burned.

So who to call for a cup of coffee and a bout of window shopping? Not Alice, because Amanda might feel left out. And certainly none of the guys from work, who repeatedly excluded her from group outings, whether because she was a woman or because she was dating the boss.

Crap. She needed more friends. Preferably female, so she could talk to them about the frustration of texting a boy and having him ignore her.

She stared at her phone, lying idly on the coffee table, and jumped when it rang.

Brad's name and picture appeared on the screen.

"Oh, thank God," she said in lieu of a greeting.

"What happened? You okay?"

"I'm fine. Just bored out of my mind. What do people do when they don't work on a weekday and can't get laid? And don't say masturbate. My arm's about to fall off."

Brad let out that sexy, throaty laugh she couldn't get enough of. "You could clean up the house."

"That's what has my arm — both arms — hurting."

"Daytime TV?"

"Eh, I guess it's my only option. Unless my loving boyfriend wants to join me for lunch."

"I think he's dying to do so. That was why he called, actually."

She cheered up at that. "Pick me up at one?"

"Two. Need to sort out some things for tomorrow."

Her curiosity was piqued. "Oh. Did ya forget to order the cake?"

"You're not getting a word out of me. Be ready at two. I'm thinking picnic."

"I'm thinking you have good thoughts."

* * * *

Becca pulled on her most colorful sundress and hopped into a pair of flats. Her checkered picnic blanket was already rolled up and in her carryall, together with a bottle of white wine. They could stop at a deli on the way to the Golden Gate Park and stock up on sandwiches. She craved some pepperoni. And maybe brie.

Her phone blipped with a text.

I'm downstairs. Take your time.

Didn't the man know her by now? She was never late when food was at stake.

Brad leaned on his car, a beaming smile on his face. She stood on tiptoe to kiss him, and he opened the door for her and took her bag. "Your chariot awaits, my lady."

"Oh, thank you, kind sir." She gave a small curtsy and folded herself into the passenger seat. She loved seeing him so relaxed. No-tie was a good look on him.

He stowed her bag in the back, got behind the wheel, and started the engine. He insisted on driving stick, and she loved it when he rested his hand on her thigh between changing gears.

"Have you already picked up food? 'Cause I was thinking of stopping by that—"

"It's all taken care of."

"I hope there's brie involved."

"I'm afraid not, but there's chocolate." He slid his hand higher on her thigh, until his fingertips touched her panty line. She'd actually worn underwear for a change; she didn't want a breeze in the park to end up traumatizing any kids because she liked going commando.

She looked at the street ahead. The bright sunlight made the pavement shine. "It's a gorgeous day for a picnic. Kickass idea."

"Are you excited about tomorrow?" Brad's question was out of left field.

"More than you know. Are you?"

"More than I thought possible."

"Sure you don't want to back out?"

"A thousand percent."

"Good." She caressed his neck, but snapped her head to the side when she caught a glimpse of a tall blond man on the sidewalk. He ducked into an entryway, and she lost him.

Brad turned right and pulled into an underground parking. With a start, Becca realized they were half a block from the building she'd been painting last week. The one she and Brad had lured Colin to. "Why are we here?" she asked.

"This is where we're eating."

Curiouser and curiouser. "The bistro? I thought you said we were going for a picnic."

"We are. At the apartment." He parked, jumped out of the car, and all but pulled her door off its hinges. "Come on."

She let him guide her outside and to the building in which she and Colin had sex last Friday. The stupid place had no elevator, and she was glad she hadn't worn heels. The bejeweled sandals were coming with her in a bag tomorrow; she'd wear her sneakers to tackle the stairs. Brad held her hand as they reached the third floor landing—a million years later.

Something was amiss, and it wasn't that she couldn't catch her breath. "My bag. You didn't get my bag. I have a blanket and wine," she said.

"I told you I have everything covered."

"*We* have everything covered," Colin said from the apartment's doorway.

"Were you waiting behind the door, for me to feed you a line?" Brad asked him.

"Nah. I just have a knack for making an entrance."

Becca looked from one to the other, confused. "What is this?"

"Your birthday party," Colin said.

"We decided to make it a surprise one." Brad nudged her toward the apartment.

"Surprise." Colin pressed against her and claimed her lips in a kiss that, when he stepped back, left her more breathless than the staircase had.

"How…?" Why was she bothering with stupid questions, when she could be kissing him again?

"He called me." Brad cupped her breast and kneaded, his tongue trailing the seam of her lips.

Colin moved further into the apartment and pulled her with him. Brad followed them and kicked the door shut.

Chapter Twenty-Four

It was happening. It was happening now instead of tomorrow. She had no makeup on, her hair was in a haphazard ponytail, and this dress was too loud for the pale yellow walls around her. It was all wrong. Nothing like she'd planned it.

But they were both there with her.

"You called Brad," she managed to say as Colin tugged her to him for another kiss.

"I wanted to make sure he was really okay with everything. That he didn't…" His gaze darkened with something other than desire, and Becca felt compelled to cup his ass.

"That he was on board?" she asked.

He removed her hand and clasped both her wrists between them. "Yes. And that the two of you knew what this would mean. I'm not going to step back gallantly if we do this, Becca. I'm not going to go quietly into the night, if you and your Mr. Right decide you've had enough fun and want to settle down. Get married. Have kids."

"I don't want these things." She tried to break his hold, but it was made of steel.

"Not now. Maybe someday."

She knew where he was coming from, but her own intimacy issues had threatened her relationship with Brad this week, and she wouldn't allow Colin's to do the same. "I can't live with maybes." This time she broke free and fisted her hands in his shirt to crash her lips to his.

Brad, who'd remained silent this long, pressed against her back and kissed her neck. "I told him, but he probably wants it in writing."

"Ass." Colin inched one finger under the strap of her dress. The bodice had built-in cups, so there was nothing covering her breast when he lowered the strap down her arm. "Fuck. These nipples haunt my dreams." He sucked on one distended peak until it was so hard it hurt.

Brad caressed her thigh, driving the loose skirt of her dress ever higher.

Had she at least worn her black lace boyshorts? She couldn't remember. Colin trailed his fingers up her inner thigh, and she stopped caring.

Brad's palm was warm on her ass, his fingers searching. He slid them under her thong—right, it was a thong—and with a harsh tug snapped the elastic band.

"Good idea." Colin bunched the other side in his hand, yanked, and her underwear was nothing but a slip of fabric on the floor.

Brad laughed. "I have more where that came from." He ran both hands up Becca's thighs until the dress was bunched around her waist, and Colin helped her take it the rest of the way up and off.

Her breasts bounced free, and warm air met the slickness between her legs. She felt lightheaded and closed her eyes, losing herself in the sensations the two men evoked. Inquisitive fingers lit every inch of her skin on fire. Her breasts. Her belly. Her buttocks.

If Brad and Colin didn't hold her up, pressed between their bodies, she'd collapse under the overwhelming pleasure.

The hands got bolder. From feathering along her thigh to brushing her nether lips. Sliding between them to tap her clit. Someone pushed a finger inside her pussy. She thought it was Brad, but when she covered the hand with hers, it felt more like Colin's.

A second finger. Someone pinched her nipple with enough force to make her cry out. She spun and moved between them, seeking more of their attentions. Brad knelt in front of her. She felt his breath on her wet skin before his tongue traced her pussy. The fingers inside her were unrelenting, their thrusts deeper as Brad ate her out.

She dug her fingers in his hair and held on for dear life, while Colin fucked her with his fingers.

"So good," she whispered. "So good."

Colin bit her ass, and she laughed. This was nothing like she'd planned. She had no control over it, but it felt incredible.

When Colin withdrew his fingers, she let out an indignant, *hey.*

"Don't worry, princess. I'm not going anywhere. Except back here." He pressed a finger to her asshole, and she bucked against Brad. She knew the night would involve things going up her ass, but she hadn't been touched there in a while. She knew Brad wanted to try it. Maybe he and Colin should change places?

Brad clasped her ass with both hands and spread the cheeks, all but presenting her to Colin, who wasted no time pushing his finger inside. Just the tip. Just enough to make her legs buckle. "I can't... Need to..." Whatever it was, words eluded her.

Colin stood and held her to him. His belt buckle was cold against her back. "Open your eyes," he said. "See how gorgeous he is."

She lifted eyelids heavy with lust, to see Brad taking off his shirt. As always, the sight of his chiseled stomach and chest made her mouth water. Gorgeous. Stunning. And hers.

This was the moment to take control. He was baring himself to her and Colin and becoming as vulnerable as she was.

She slipped out of Colin's arms. By the time she tiptoed to Brad, his shirt lay in a heap on the floor, and he was fumbling with his belt. "Let me get that." Becca undid the buckle, and slowly pulled the belt out of its loops, grazing his chest with her hardened nipples. She was acutely aware of Colin watching, as she went down on her knees and shoved Brad's slacks down his legs.

Brad closed his hands over her shoulders and lifted her to her feet. "Today is about you. Enjoy it."

Becca considered arguing but saw no reason to. She turned to Colin. "You. Too many clothes. Get with the program."

He gave her a wicked smirk, pants already around his hips. "Last chance to back out."

"No backing out," Brad said.

Becca nodded. She couldn't speak, because Colin's magnificent cock was interfering with her cognitive process. She caught herself licking her lips. Heat crept up her neck and spread to her cheeks.

Colin's smirk morphed into a gleeful smile that made her stomach flutter. "I made you blush," he said with a chuckle.

"Shut up." But she was laughing too, and so was Brad.

"She's an innocent little girl, don't you know?" Brad asked.

She spun his way and tickled him, and he lifted her in his arms and walked backward until he landed in an armchair, Becca on top of him. What was the armchair even doing there? The apartment wasn't furnished.

She filed the question for a later time.

Still laughing, she lifted her face to his, and the lust burning in his dark brown eyes killed the sound in her throat. Holding his gaze, she spread her legs, positioned him at her entrance, and lowered her body. Inch by inch, she took him in, relishing the pressure inside as much as the anticipation. He fit her perfectly, and she didn't want to hold back. She wanted to ride him hard and chase her orgasm. She didn't. She wanted to feel every move, be present in the moment, until the moment was all there was.

He sank inside her to the hilt, and she let out a sigh. This was where she belonged. This was heaven. She lifted her hips a fraction at a time, until only the tip of his cock remained inside her, and then began taking him all in again. She couldn't keep that rhythm for long, though, and not because her thighs burned with exertion. She wasn't good with self-restraint. She wanted to come. She wanted Colin too. She looked over her shoulder, where he pulled on his cock. Paler than Brad's and slightly less thick but just as long, it glistened with precum or spit as the head disappeared inside his fist only to appear again a second later.

"Colin." She wasn't sure her voice carried, but he looked at her with the same wild desire Brad did, and she wanted him too. Now.

He approached unhurriedly, allowing her to admire the sleek, long muscles of his body. His movements had a feline grace and yet were nothing if not masculine. His presence filled the room, and Becca wanted him to fill her.

She leaned forward and draped her body over Brad's. Brad folded an arm across her shoulders, and reached down to grab her ass with his other hand.

The blunt tip of Colin's cock pressed against her asshole, and she clenched instinctively. She wasn't ready. He hadn't prepared her.

Colin rubbed soothing circles at the small of her back, but he didn't stop pressing forward. "Relax into it," he said.

There was a cock inside her already. Maybe her body couldn't fit another. "*You* relax into it."

"Maybe later."

Brad laughed, and she laughed, and Colin drove past the tight ring of muscle.

"Once the head is in, it gets easier," he said.

"I know." She was getting irritated. She wasn't supposed to be irritated. Why had Brad stopped moving?

She looked down at him and was captivated by the raw need in his eyes, as he watched Colin. Brad was as into this — as into Colin — as she was. He'd said he wanted Colin, but seeing it was different, and infinitely sexy.

"I want to see you kiss," she said. "Please."

Brad gave her a lazy smile, and turned his face up for Colin to find his lips over Becca's shoulder. For the first time, she was grateful for her five-foot-four.

"I'm going to ask for more of this later."

Brad let his head fall back again. "Anytime."

Becca dipped in for a kiss and tasted Colin. She reached behind her, threw an arm around Colin's neck, and brought him to her for another kiss. He cupped her breasts and pinched the nipples. Rolled them until a moan tore through their kiss.

She rubbed her cheek against his, and pushed back, taking in more of his cock. It burned, but the worst part was that it kept her mind working, when she didn't want to be thinking.

Brad solved that problem. "How does it feel, having both of us dying to fuck you? Knowing you have us. We're yours." His voice was even lower than usual. Gruffer. It sent a shiver rolling down her spine.

He pumped his hips, and she met his thrust. Colin pushed harder this time.

"Fuck." Becca felt impossibly stretched even before Colin was fully seated inside her ass. Her eyes stung, and her skin was on fire.

Then Colin withdrew as Brad pushed in, and the pain stopped being an issue. She still throbbed, but with a fierce need. They moved again, perfectly synchronized, as if they'd always done this, and Becca let them carry her on a wave of sensation that threatened to drown her at the same time it promised to lift her to the skies and give her wings to soar. Could she die of pleasure overload?

She licked Brad's neck, tasted the salt of his sweat. The clean scent of Colin's aftershave or shower gel surrounded her. Two hard cocks pistoned inside her.

If she'd die right there, she'd go happy.

"Incredible. Fucking incredible." Colin spread her ass cheeks with his palms and dug his fingers in her flesh. She moved her hips faster, wanting him to hold on tighter. To leave bruises.

Beneath her Brad trembled. He was holding back. He should know he didn't have to. They could do this again. They *would* do it again. All the time, if she had any say in it.

Colin lost all restraint and thrust inside her in earnest, as Brad's movements became jerkier.

Her own body felt light and heavy at the same time. Exhausted and renewed. She was close and got closer with each plunge. She wedged her hand between her body and Brad's. The barest touch to her clit, and a jolt like electricity arched her back and made her legs feel like jelly.

She thrashed between the men, unable to control her limbs as ecstasy took over, sending her hurtling to her release.

She clenched around Brad and Colin, pulling them with her off the edge. Colin held out the longest, filling her with cum a few seconds after Brad was spent inside her.

"Happy birthday to me." She muffled a giggle in Brad's chest, and he ruffled her hair. Colin collapsed on top of her, echoing Brad's laugh. They rumbled against her. Through her.

Colin withdrew gently from her body and seconds later brought a wet towel to wipe her clean. They were prepared, her boys.

The divine smell of fried dough reached her nostrils. "Is there food in the room?" she asked, standing on wobbly legs.

"Yeah," Brad said.

"We were supposed to have dinner first, but we got sidetracked," Colin said.

"Is it Chinese? Say it's Chinese." Now that she'd noticed, she couldn't believe she hadn't smelled it sooner. She looked to the dining room. A moving box—taped shut and set for three, with red placemats, paper plates, and plastic cups—was laden with cartons of food. Large pillows were strewn around it, and behind it she made out a bottle of pink champagne chilling in a bucket of ice. It was her special-occasion drink.

Masking her smile beneath a pout, she asked, "But what are we going to do tomorrow, for my actual birthday?"

"A repeat?" Brad smacked her ass on his way to the makeshift table.

Colin tangled his fingers with hers and led her to the smorgasbord they'd laid out for her. "If you can take us both again so soon, that is." He helped her lower her sore body to one of the plumpest pillows, sat to her right, and winked at Brad, who made himself comfortable across from him.

"I'm willing to try. You planned every little detail, huh?" She pointed at the armchair with her chopsticks.

Brad shook his head. "Actually, this was a gift with the huge-ass bed we had delivered this morning. We meant to take you in the bedroom. *After* dinner."

"We still have to. The guys who carried the bed upstairs cursed us repeatedly. Can't let that be in vain," Colin said.

Becca tried to keep a straight face and failed. "Well then, we'll have to break it in. Honor their hard work."

They dug in, occasionally exchanging touches, looks, or jibes. Becca kept expecting things to get weird. Awkward. They didn't. The champagne and conversation flowed, and soon she found herself planning tomorrow. A series of tomorrows. Maybe some of them would involve her pretty boys kissing and fucking while she gave directions. Yeah, she'd like that.

She leaned in to kiss Colin and gave Brad's cock a playful tug. They'd need to start wearing clothes to dinner, or they'd never finish a meal.

She stuck a won ton in her mouth and grinned around it. She couldn't wait for the next round.

And there was chocolate.

Epilogue

Becca woke up sore and sated.

Brad and Colin spent the night playing her body like a fiddle. They took her again and again until all three of them collapsed in a heap on the bed. Like every night.

She fucking loved her life, and her boys.

This three-way dating thing was fun, though they still hadn't attended any get-togethers with friends and family as an item. Their tastes ran similar, and with three votes on everything, there was never a stalemate.

And the sex… *God.* She stretched languidly in all directions, expecting to feel the bodies of her lovers on either side. Funny how they'd agreed they didn't need to be all together all the time, yet hadn't slept apart for weeks, even when they didn't have sex.

Her fingers touched cool sheets, and she cracked an eyelid open. She was alone in bed, the pale pink light of early morning sun filtering in through the curtains and painting shadows on the walls. The huge windows in this place were gorgeous, but Brad insisted on curtains when he moved in. She still couldn't believe the apartment that housed their first trysts with Colin now belonged to Brad. Good thing she adored it, since she'd practically moved in. She and Colin both had. They kept their places, but barely ever visited them—in Becca's case, to check her mail and pretend she wasn't tamed by love.

Which she totally was. But how come no one was in bed with her? "Brad? Colin?"

Ms. Thing lay sprawled in the armchair at the corner. The cat didn't bat an eyelash. She seemed as exhausted as Becca felt. How were the boys able to stand after the previous night, let alone walk out of the room?

The sound of running water reached her ears. Shower. That was a good idea. She briefly wondered if she'd find Colin or Brad in the bathroom. The two avoided being naked together when she didn't act as a buffer between them. It was odd after what they shared—her, namely—on a near-nightly basis.

She joked about the two of them fucking while she watched, and saw the longing in Colin's gaze when Brad wasn't looking. Brad confessed he just needed time, but he remained silent when Colin joked about giving him head, to get him used to the idea.

When she was between them, there was no hesitation in their touch. They explored each other's body as well as hers, and they kissed with a hunger that drove her wild with desire. It never went further than that.

They wanted each other. They admitted it. They'd taken the first steps. Why not give in? Becca would have to get them to move things along.

But first, she'd hop in the shower with whichever of them cared to keep her company.

She groaned as she stood. Her pussy felt tender and raw, and her hamstrings had muscle fever. Sex was off the table tonight, but she wouldn't say no to being massaged and eaten out under the water jet.

She moved gingerly to the bathroom, but her naked feet slid on the hardwood floor. Her momentum almost brought her head-first through the door, as she skidded to a halt at the sight before her.

Brad was buried inside Colin to the hilt, and they both seemed to love it. Of course there was nothing *not* to love, from where she stood.

Becca was so happy they hadn't bothered to slide the shower door shut. With the steam in the room, she wouldn't be able to see a thing through the glass. And there was so much yummy male flesh to see.

Hard, toned bodies pushed against each other, muscles flexing and rippling. Their groans and grunts were drowned under the rush of pelting water, but she thought she heard the slapping of flesh against flesh. She wanted to hear it. Wanted to be close enough to touch them. But this wasn't about her.

Brad had his large palms splayed on Colin's hips, holding him in place as he hammered inside him.

Colin leaned his head on the wall, one hand clawing at the slippery tiles, the other pulling on his cock. Eyes closed, he pushed back, meeting every one of Brad's thrusts.

Becca cautiously moved a little to the side, to absorb every detail of their coupling. The room grew hotter with every breath, her desire for the two men rising.

Brad's face was pinched in concentration, his movements measured, as though he was afraid he'd hurt Colin. *No.* As if he wasn't sure what he did was right. But it was. The proof was in the silent *O* Colin's lips formed every time Brad's hips slammed against his ass, the thick cock disappearing inside him.

Becca knew how that felt. She had Brad inside her hours earlier and could still feel the double pounding her beautiful boys gave her.

Beautiful.

Soap suds and water didn't mask the striking contrast of Colin's golden skin against Brad's tan. Brad's wet dark hair clung to his face, while Colin's short blond spikes stood upright, defying water and gravity. So different and yet both so perfect.

Steam rose around them, framing them in misty halos, but they were no angels. She wouldn't want them this much if they were.

Becca palmed her breast and kneaded it. The nipple stood erect, and she pinched it hard, swallowing a moan. She couldn't bother with foreplay; she was soaking wet and throbbing with need. She glided her hand down her bare stomach and to the apex of her thighs. She pushed her fingers inside her folds and circled her clitoris. Rubbed. Hard. Fast.

She was still sore, but pleasure overrode pain, as she hurtled toward her orgasm. The sight in front of her, her fingers still torturing her flesh, and the musky scent of Brad's shower gel made her head light. She slid down the wall till her ass met the cold floor.

As she watched, Colin straightened his body, and Brad wrapped both arms around him. Pinning Colin in place, Brad jerked his hips in short thrusts until his roar of release covered every other sound.

Colin pulled away as soon as Brad loosened his hold. He turned to face Brad, grabbed him by the back of the neck, and crashed their mouths together. He said something Becca didn't make out, and they turned so Brad's back was to the wall, Colin between his thighs.

Colin tugged on his cock and rubbed it against Brad's stomach. He bit along Brad's jaw line, and said something else she didn't catch. Or maybe he kissed Brad's ear.

Brad batted Colin's hand away and closed his fist around Colin's cock. He pulled at him until Colin's cum sprayed his arm and stomach, and was washed away. They kissed again, laughing. No awkwardness. Just glee.

Becca wanted to be included in their moment. Could she join them in the shower, or shouldn't she have witnessed something this private? Was it a spur-of-the-moment thing, while she happened to be asleep, or did they mean to hide it from her?

Only one way to find out. She stood and pushed the door all the way open. "Can I join you in there, or is this shower a male-bonding-only area now?"

Colin laughed. He did that a lot these days, and it suited him. Brad blushed, but he grinned and held out a hand for her.

Yeah, Becca fucking loved her life.

The End

Keep up to date with all the latest news and information from Sotia Lazu at http://www.SotiaLazu.com

Acknowledgments

Thank you, Allyson Lindt and Sofia Grey, for not letting me leave this story unfinished. For beta-reading and tossing me ideas and making time for Colin and Brad and Becca in your hectic schedules.

Thank you all who read *Colin* when it was a separate novella, and asked for more.

Thank you, Andrei, for reading even the parts you weren't happy with. I love you.

About the Author

Sotia loves romances with a twist and urban fantasy novels, always with vivid erotic elements. Her favorite characters to write are not conventional hero-material at first glance, and she enjoys making them fight for their happiness.

She shares her life and living quarters with her husband, their son, and two rescue dogs, one of which may be part-pony. Sappy movies make her bawl like a baby, and she wishes she could take in all the stray dogs in the world.

Also, she hates mornings!

www.ingramcontent.com/pod-product-compliance
Lightning Source LLC
Chambersburg PA
CBHW072227190626
46809CB00017B/1006